QUARRELITE

Power Crystal

Once a Star Darling has granted her first wish and returns to Starland, she receives a very special treasure—a beautiful Power Crystal.

WRISTBANDS

Wish Pendant

A Wish Pendant is a powerful accessory worn by a Star Darling. On Wishworld, it helps her identify her Wisher and stores the ever-important wish energy.

Astra's Mixed-Up Mission

Astra's Mixed-Up Mission

Shana Muldoon Zappa and Ahmet Zappa
with Zelda Rose

Disney Press

Los Angeles • New York

Copyright © 2016 Disney Enterprises, Inc.

All rights reserved. Published by Disney Press, an imprint of Disney
Book Group. No part of this book may be reproduced or transmitted
in any form or by any means, electronic or mechanical, including
photocopying, recording, or by any information storage and retrieval
system, without written permission from the publisher.
For information address Disney Press,
1101 Flower Street, Glendale, California 91201.

Printed in the United States of America
Reinforced Binding
First Paperback Edition, April 2016
1 3 5 7 9 10 8 6 4 2

FAC-025438-16050

Library of Congress Control Number: 2015958596
ISBN 978-1-4847-1427-0

For more Disney Press fun, visit www.disneybooks.com

Halo Violetta Zappa. You are pure light, joy, and inspiration. We love you soooooo much.

May the Star Darlings continue to shine brightly upon you. May every step upon your path be blessed with positivity and the understanding that you have the power within you to manifest the most fulfilling life you can possibly dream of and more. May you always remember that being different and true to yourself makes your inner star shine brighter. And never ever stop making wishes.

Glow for it. . . .
Mommy and Daddy

And to everyone else here on "Wishworld":

May you realize that no matter where you are in life, no matter what you look like or where you were born, you, too, have the power within you to create the life of your dreams. Through celebrating your own uniqueness, thinking positively, and taking action, you can make your wishes come true. May you understand that you are never alone. There is always someone near who will understand you if you look hard enough. The Star Darlings are here to remind you that there is an unstoppable energy to staying positive, wishing, and believing in yourself. That inner star shines within you.

Smile. The Star Darlings have your back. We know how startastic you truly are.

Glow for it. . . .
Your friends,
Shana and Ahmet

Student Reports

NAME: Clover
BRIGHT DAY: January 5
FAVORITE COLOR: Purple
INTERESTS: Music, painting, studying
WISH: To be the best songwriter and DJ on Starland
WHY CHOSEN: Clover has great self-discipline, patience, and willpower. She is creative, responsible, dependable, and extremely loyal.
WATCH OUT FOR: Clover can be hard to read and she is reserved with those she doesn't know. She's afraid to take risks and can be a wisecracker at times.
SCHOOL YEAR: Second
POWER CRYSTAL: Panthera
WISH PENDANT: Barrette

NAME: Adora
BRIGHT DAY: February 14
FAVORITE COLOR: Sky blue
INTERESTS: Science, thinking about the future and how she can make it better
WISH: To be the top fashion designer on Starland
WHY CHOSEN: Adora is clever and popular and cares about the world around her. She's a deep thinker.
WATCH OUT FOR: Adora can have her head in the clouds and be thinking about other things.
SCHOOL YEAR: Third
POWER CRYSTAL: Azurica
WISH PENDANT: Watch

NAME: Piper
BRIGHT DAY: March 4
FAVORITE COLOR: Seafoam green
INTERESTS: Composing poetry and writing in her dream journal
WISH: To become the best version of herself she can possibly be and to share that by writing books
WHY CHOSEN: Piper is giving, kind, and sensitive. She is very intuitive and aware.
WATCH OUT FOR: Piper can be dreamy, absentminded, and wishy-washy. She can also be moody and easily swayed by the opinions of others.
SCHOOL YEAR: Second
POWER CRYSTAL: Dreamalite
WISH PENDANT: Bracelets

Starling Academy

NAME: Astra
BRIGHT DAY: April 9
FAVORITE COLOR: Red
INTERESTS: Individual sports
WISH: To be the best athlete on Starland—to win!
WHY CHOSEN: Astra is energetic, brave, clever, and confident. She has boundless energy and is always direct and to the point.
WATCH OUT FOR: Astra is sometimes cocky, self-centered, condescending, and brash.
SCHOOL YEAR: Second
POWER CRYSTAL: Quarrelite
WISH PENDANT: Wristbands

••••*••*••*

NAME: Tessa
BRIGHT DAY: May 18
FAVORITE COLOR: Emerald green
INTERESTS: Food, flowers, love
WISH: To be successful enough that she can enjoy a life of luxury
WHY CHOSEN: Tessa is warm, charming, affectionate, trustworthy, and dependable. She has incredible drive and commitment.
WATCH OUT FOR: Tessa does not like to be rushed. She can be quite stubborn and often says no. She does not deal well with change and is prone to exaggeration. She can be easily sidetracked.
SCHOOL YEAR: Third
POWER CRYSTAL: Gossamer
WISH PENDANT: Brooch

••••*••*••*

NAME: Gemma
BRIGHT DAY: June 2
FAVORITE COLOR: Orange
INTERESTS: Sharing her thoughts about almost anything
WISH: To be valued for her opinions on everything
WHY CHOSEN: Gemma is friendly, easygoing, funny, extroverted, and social. She knows a little bit about everything.
WATCH OUT FOR: Gemma talks—a lot—and can be a little too honest sometimes and offend others. She can have a short attention span and can be superficial.
SCHOOL YEAR: First
POWER CRYSTAL: Scatterite
WISH PENDANT: Earrings

Student Reports

NAME: Cassie
BRIGHT DAY: July 6
FAVORITE COLOR: White
INTERESTS: Reading, crafting
WISH: To be more independent and confident and less fearful
WHY CHOSEN: Cassie is extremely imaginative and artistic. She is a voracious reader and is loyal, caring, and a good friend. She is very intuitive.
WATCH OUT FOR: Cassie can be distrustful, jealous, moody, and brooding.
SCHOOL YEAR: First
POWER CRYSTAL: Lunalite
WISH PENDANT: Glasses

NAME: Leona
BRIGHT DAY: August 16
FAVORITE COLOR: Gold
INTERESTS: Acting, performing, dressing up
WISH: To be the most famous pop star on Starland
WHY CHOSEN: Leona is confident, hardworking, generous, open-minded, optimistic, caring, and a strong leader.
WATCH OUT FOR: Leona can be vain, opinionated, selfish, bossy, dramatic, and stubborn and is prone to losing her temper.
SCHOOL YEAR: Third
POWER CRYSTAL: Glisten paw
WISH PENDANT: Cuff

NAME: Vega
BRIGHT DAY: September 1
FAVORITE COLOR: Blue
INTERESTS: Exercising, analyzing, cleaning, solving puzzles
WISH: To be the top student at Starling Academy
WHY CHOSEN: Vega is reliable, observant, organized, and very focused.
WATCH OUT FOR: Vega can be opinionated about everything, and she can be fussy, uptight, critical, arrogant, and easily embarrassed.
SCHOOL YEAR: Second
POWER CRYSTAL: Queezle
WISH PENDANT: Belt

Starling Academy

NAME: Libby
BRIGHT DAY: October 12
FAVORITE COLOR: Pink
INTERESTS: Helping others, interior design, art, dancing
WISH: To give everyone what they need—both on Starland and through wish granting on Wishworld
WHY CHOSEN: Libby is generous, articulate, gracious, diplomatic, and kind.
WATCH OUT FOR: Libby can be indecisive and may try too hard to please everyone.
SCHOOL YEAR: First
POWER CRYSTAL: Charmelite
WISH PENDANT: Necklace

NAME: Scarlet
BRIGHT DAY: November 3
FAVORITE COLOR: Black
INTERESTS: Crystal climbing (and other extreme sports), magic, thrill seeking
WISH: To live on Wishworld
WHY CHOSEN: Scarlet is confident, intense, passionate, magnetic, curious, and very brave.
WATCH OUT FOR: Scarlet is a loner and can alienate others by being secretive, arrogant, stubborn, and jealous.
SCHOOL YEAR: Third
POWER CRYSTAL: Ravenstone
WISH PENDANT: Boots

NAME: Sage
BRIGHT DAY: December 1
FAVORITE COLOR: Lavender
INTERESTS: Travel, adventure, telling stories, nature, and philosophy
WISH: To become the best Wish-Granter Starland has ever seen
WHY CHOSEN: Sage is honest, adventurous, curious, optimistic, friendly, and relaxed.
WATCH OUT FOR: Sage has a quick temper! She can also be restless, irresponsible, and too trusting of others' opinions. She may jump to conclusions.
SCHOOL YEAR: First
POWER CRYSTAL: Lavenderite
WISH PENDANT: Necklace

Introduction

You take a deep breath, about to blow out the candles on your birthday cake. Clutching a coin in your fist, you get ready to toss it into the dancing waters of a fountain. You stare at your little brother as you each hold an end of a dried wishbone, about to pull. But what do you do first?

You make a wish, of course!

Ever wonder what happens right after you make that wish? *Not much*, you may be thinking.

Well, you'd be wrong.

Because something quite unexpected happens next. Each and every wish that is made becomes a glowing Wish Orb, invisible to the human eye. This undetectable orb zips through the air and into the heavens, on a one-way trip to the brightest star in the sky—a magnificent place called Starland. Starland is inhabited by Starlings, who look a lot like you and me, except they have a sparkly glow to their skin, and glittery hair in unique colors. And they have one more thing: magical powers. The Starlings use these powers to make good wishes come true, for when good wishes are granted, the result is positive energy. And the Starlings of Starland need this energy to keep their world running.

In case you are wondering, there are three kinds of Wish Orbs:

1) GOOD WISH ORBS. These wishes are positive and helpful and come from the heart. They are pretty and sparkly and are nurtured in climate-controlled Wish-Houses. They bloom into fantastical glowing orbs. When the time is right, they are presented to the appropriate Starling for wish fulfillment.

2) BAD WISH ORBS. These are for selfish, mean-spirited, or negative things. They don't sparkle

at all. They are immediately transported to a special containment center, as they are very dangerous and must not be granted.

3) IMPOSSIBLE WISH ORBS. These wishes are for things, like world peace and disease cures, that simply can't be granted by Starlings. These sparkle with an almost impossibly bright light and are taken to a special area of the Wish-House with tinted windows to contain the glare they produce. The hope is that one day they can be turned into good wishes the Starlings can help grant.

Starlings take their wish granting very seriously. There is a special school, called Starling Academy, that accepts only the best and brightest young Starling girls. They study hard for four years, and when they graduate, they are ready to start traveling to Wishworld to help grant wishes. For as long as anyone can remember, only graduates of wish-granting schools have ever been allowed to travel to Wishworld. But things have changed in a very big way.

Read on for the rest of the story. . . .

Prologue

STAR MEMORANDUM, Astra typed on her holo-keyboard.

TO: Cassie and Piper, was the next line.

Then: *FROM: Astra*

She paused for a moment as she considered the subject line. She needed to get Cassie's attention. The question was, how?

Something strange was going on at Starling Academy. Astra was almost sure of it, and Piper was pretty convinced, too. They wanted to discuss it with one of the other Star Darlings, but Astra couldn't decide whom to approach. Piper suggested talking to Cassie, mentioning her thoughtfulness and perceptiveness. And Astra was, despite her initial hesitation, learning to trust Piper's instincts. To be completely honest, when she first met Piper, she had found her slow dreaminess annoying and her occasional dark side ridiculous. But now Astra had a new respect for both the hidden messages that dreams could hold and the strength of Piper's intuitive powers.

But even though Cassie had been so concerned about the flowers, she was now completely focused on herself. She spoke about her starmazing mission, about how startacularly it had gone. She continued by praising her own wish energy manipulation skills. She even went on to discuss her eyelashes, calling them "dusky, luxurious, and starmazingly sooty." Astra could barely even see them behind those large star-shaped glasses Cassie wore, so she told her she'd have to take her word for it.

Perhaps she had snorted as she said it? Because Cassie had stormed off. Possibly to go look in a mirror. Or to find someone with a finer appreciation of eyelashes. Who knew?

So Astra decided it might be best to send both Cassie and Piper a holo-message. Something short, direct, and to the point. But what should the subject be? She thought and thought and then smiled as she came up with the perfect idea. Astra's fingers practically flew over the holo-keyboard. So many odd things had happened since the beginning of the starmester!

STAR MEMORANDUM

TO: Cassie and Piper
FROM: Astra
SUBJECT: Top ten weird things that have been going on at Starling Academy

10) MESSED-UP MISSIONS. EVERYONE. (Think about it: each and every Star Darling who has been sent down to Wishworld has had great difficulty identifying her Wisher or figuring out the wish.)

9) SCARLET'S OUSTER. (One day she was a Star Darling; the next she was kicked out. Then the Wish Orb picked her to save a mission that was going badly and she was back in the fold again. Startastically strange.)

8) POWER WENT OUT. (We've been taught since we were in Wee Constellation School that we have massive wish energy reserves. How in Starland could the lights have gone out?)

7) THE RANKER. (Somehow the whole school got invited to try out for Leona's band. The Ranker was brought in to choose the band members and their name, and it chose an all-SD band and the name of our secret group for the band. Coincidence? Perhaps not.)

6) FIGHTING FLOWERS. (Each of our rooms had a vase of these. We all fought like rats and hogs, or whatever that Wishling expression is. Now that they are gone—thanks, Cassie—we are getting along again. Something to think about.)

5) PIPER'S FOREBODING DREAMS. (No offense, Piper, but I used to think you were way creepy. Now I know you've got some stellar prediction skills.)

4) ONE WORD: OPHELIA. (It makes entirely no sense that someone so clueless could have been a real Star Darling. Then you got suspicious of her, Cassie, and she disappeared.)

3) LEONA'S FAILED MISSION. (She's self-absorbed—star apologies, Cassie—but even I felt bad when she didn't collect wish energy and her Wish Pendant got all burnt-looking. What an embarrassment.)

2) STAR KINDNESS DAY MESSAGES WERE THE EXACT OPPOSITE OF WHAT WAS INTENDED. (Because I know that neither of you think I am a bad sportswoman, or that I have slow reflexes. And no, I am not holding any grudges.)

1) EVERYONE IS ACTING LIKE A WEIRDO! (Star apologies again, Cassie, but it's true. Piper and I can't put our finger on exactly what it is, but we'll get to the bottom of this soon. . . .)

Astra smiled, read it through one more time, and pressed SEND. To her disbelief, the entire holo-document disappeared into thin air. *"Starf!"* she yelled.

The sparkle shower turned off and her roommate, Clover, stepped into the room. "Are you okay?" she asked Astra. Her eyes lit up. "Do you need a hug?" Not waiting for an answer, Clover headed her way, arms wide.

"See you at breakfast!" Astra called as she expertly dodged away from her roommate's embrace. She picked up her starstick, slid the door open smoothly using energy manipulation, and was gone.

CHAPTER
1

"Piper! Piper!" called Astra, waving urgently at the girl sitting across the cafeteria table from her. Astra's red-and-silver-striped fingernails caught the light and she noticed with dismay that the polish she had applied on Wishworld was already starting to chip. She knew it wouldn't last through Physical Energy class later that afternoon. What a difference from her Starland manicure, which had taken *forever* to remove!

Piper looked up from her dream holo-diary, flipping a lock of hair the color of ocean foam over her shoulder. "Is someone on the way?" she asked.

"I think Tessa is heading over," Astra told her. After striking out with Cassie, they had tried to talk to some of the other Star Darlings and had begun to notice that something seemed off with each and every one of them. But they couldn't figure out exactly what was going on. So they decided they'd study their roommates first and report to each other.

Back in their room, after Clover had hugged Astra tightly for the tenth time, she realized that no one could possibly have missed her that much. So she sent Piper a holo-text:

 Clover is a mad hugger! What about Vega?

After a while she received a holo-text:

 To figure it out took me some time. But Vega only talks in rhyme!

They made plans to study the rest of the Star Darlings the next starday, starting at breakfast. So there they sat, awaiting their arrival.

Piper shut off the dream diary with a swipe of her hand. "Star apologies, Astra," she said. "I just thought I'd skim through some of my latest dream entries to see if I could come up with any clues about what's going on. You know, any themes or symbols that might have deeper meaning."

Just a few stardays earlier, Astra would have scoffed at such a statement. But now she totally got it.

"Find anything?" Astra asked hopefully.

Piper sighed. "Not yet," she said.

They both watched as Tessa, her brilliant green eyes flashing, made a glitterbeeline for the table near the windows that the Star Darlings had claimed as their own. All the Star Darlings knew how much Tessa loved food and looked forward to each meal. "Star greetings," she said pleasantly. She plopped down in a chair. "I'm starving!" she announced.

A Bot-Bot waiter zoomed up to drop off Piper's and Astra's breakfasts and take Tessa's order. She thought for a moment, then nodded. "I'll take a pastry basket and a cup of Zing, please," she said.

Her breakfast arrived shortly thereafter. Tessa's hand hovered over the baked treats, and she licked her lips as she made her choice. She pulled out an ozzief-ruit croissant and took a big bite. "Moonberry," she said when she was done chewing. She made quick work of the flaky pastry, then, dabbing the corners of her mouth with a cloth napkin for any errant crumbs, reached in again. This time she grabbed a mini astromuffin, which Astra could see was liberally studded with lolofruit. She popped the entire thing into her mouth and chewed.

"Moonberry again!" she said. "What are the chances?"

Astra's Star-Zap, which was sitting in her lap in silent mode, flickered. She flipped it open and read the message.

 Tessa = Everything tastes like moonberries?

 Sure looks that way!

Cassie and Sage strolled in next. Cassie sat next to Piper and smiled at her as she flicked open her napkin.

"Starkudos on your mission, Piper," she said.

"Star salutations, Cassie," Piper said, digging into her bowl of Quasar Krispies with sliced starberries.

"It probably didn't . . ." Cassie began, obviously trying to figure out the best way to phrase her statement. "It probably didn't go quite as seamlessly as mine, did it?" She thought for a moment and laughed, placing a hand on Piper's arm. "Of course it didn't," she said. "What was I thinking? My mission was such a stellar success!"

Piper looked stricken for a moment. But her expression changed to a knowing grin when she received Astra's holo-text:

 Cassie = Braggy! Now her weird behavior yesterday makes sense!

The rest of the Star Darlings began to arrive at the table. Astra and Piper watched as Sage giggled when Clover shamefacedly confessed to getting a D (for *dim*) on her Chronicle Class examination and then guffawed when the Bot-Bot waiter informed her that the kitchen was out of the Sparkle-O's she had ordered.

 Sage = Can't stop laughing.

Piper nodded and began to compose a holo-message in response.

 Libby = Can't stay awake.

Astra looked at the girl, whose cheek was resting on her plate of tinsel toast. *My stars*, she thought. She reached for her mug, drank the last gulp of twinkle tea, and began to compose a reply.

"Hey," said Cassie, noticing. "Are you writing a message about me?" She looked down at her silver dress and lace tights and smiled. "I did pick a startastically fashionable outfit this morning, didn't I?"

Astra wanted to roll her eyes but instead replied (as pleasantly as she could), "You *do* look nice today."

They don't know that they are acting odd, do they?

 I don't think so. Let's see. . . .

"Vega," Piper said, "have you noticed that everything you say is in rhyme?"

Ten Star Darlings swiveled around to look at Piper, curious expressions on their faces.

Cassie cocked her head to the side. "Really?" she said. "I don't hear it."

Gemma turned to Tessa. "Imagine if I talked in rhyme all the time. That would be so annoying!"

Tessa laughed. "My stars!" she said to her sister. "Bite your tongue!"

"Ouch!" said Gemma.

Astra made a mental note, to be verified later. *Gemma = Takes things literally?*

Vega stared at Piper like she had three auras. "Piper, do you need some schooling? Talking in rhyme? You must be fooling!"

With a quick glance at Astra, Piper asked, "You really didn't just hear that?"

"I think it is completely clear," Vega replied. "There isn't anything to hear."

Does that answer your question?

 It certainly does!

Soon it was time to head to class. Piper and Astra lingered at the table as the rest of the Star Darlings gathered their Star-Zaps and stood up to leave. Their Bot-Bot waiter collected the breakfast utensils and dishes around them.

"Star salutations, SL-D9," said Astra. When he zoomed off, she turned to Piper. "It's just so startastically strange that no one knows they are acting odd."

Piper nodded. "Or that anyone else is, either," she added.

The two girls headed out of the cafeteria, down the steps, and toward Halo Hall.

Suddenly, Piper grabbed Astra's arm and jerked her backward. "Watch out!" she cried. Astra realized that she had almost been knocked down by a Starling rushing to class.

Astra stared after her. "Was that Scarlet?" she said.

Piper nodded.

"And was she *skipping*?" Astra asked incredulously.

"She was skipping," said Piper.

"Well, now I've seen everything," said Astra. "We've got to figure this weirdness out, and fast."

"So why aren't *we* acting odd?" asked Piper.

"Great question," said Astra. "I think when we sort out that part, we'll be able to get to the bottom of this."

Piper sighed. "Let's figure it out soon," she said. "If I have to listen to Vega's rhymes for much longer, I think I'll scream!"

CHAPTER
2

"Ahhhhhhhhhhhhhhhhhhhhhhhhhhhhhhhhh!"
shrieked Piper.

Vega jumped, then turned to Piper, her brow furrowed in concern. "Piper, are you quite all right?" she asked. "Your screaming gave me such a fright."

Piper's mouth opened as if she might yelp again, and Astra put a steadying hand on her arm. Vega, who had just bumped into the two girls on her way to class, shook her head in consternation and headed down the hallway, glancing back over her shoulder worriedly at Piper.

Piper turned to Astra and gave her a shaky smile. "My sincerest star apologies," she said. "But I just can't stand the rhyming anymore."

"No star apologies necessary," said Astra. "Really. I get it. Everyone's behavior is not just weird, it is star-tastically annoying. We'll figure it out after SD class this afternoon," she told Piper, more confidently than she felt. "I'll see you later. I'm off to Aspirational Art."

Piper brightened. "Maybe it will spark some creative ideas," she said hopefully.

Astra shrugged. "Doubtful. I don't even know why I have to take Aspirational Art, anyway," she said. "I'd much rather do a double P.E. class." Astra ignored Piper's shudder. She knew that while Piper loved stretching and meditating, she was no fan of team sports.

Astra walked into the classroom, a huge airy space with beautiful light pouring through the floor-to-ceiling windows. Giant holo-canvases, one for each student, were set up around the room. Each had an artist's station furnished with brushes of all sizes and tubs of glowing paintlight in every color of the rainbow. Astra selected a canvas positioned in the corner, which overlooked the lush ozziefruit orchard.

The rest of the students began choosing their canvases, ready to begin. But where was their professor?

"Should we just start?" asked Fioney, a girl with bright blue curls. She picked up a brush and positioned it over her jar of purple paintlight, eager to get started.

Astra grinned as she observed the empty doorway. "Maybe he's not coming and we'll get a free period!" she said hopefully.

Gaila, a serious girl with a turquoise aura, gasped. "We need to stay, Astra," she gently chided. "Imagine if he came in and we were all gone!"

Astra eyed the holo-clock. "If he's not here by eleven-eighty, I say we make our starry way elsewhere," she said. "We could all go for a run. Or play a game of Poses!"

"Or take a nap!" said a girl named Smilla, who had a bright green buzz cut. The rest of the class laughed.

Half the class stared at the holo-clock and the other half stared at the door as the starmins ticked by. With ten starsecs to go before eleven-eighty, the door slid open with a bang and Professor Findley Claxworth stood there, his tall frame filling the doorway. Astra sighed. "Sorry I'm late!" he said, his purple hair in even more disarray than usual. "But I couldn't find my favorite pair of purple socks! And you know how much I love to match." He indicated his purple-and-turquoise striped shirt.

"Did you find them?" asked Smilla.

"Yes, to my great relief!" he said with a grin as he lifted his pant leg to show everyone his violet socks.

The door slid shut behind him as he stepped inside

the classroom. "I hope you girls are ready to let your creativity soar today," he announced. "Today is going to be all about letting go of your inhibitions and shining like the creative geniuses I know you are. Today you should all just go crazy!"

Astra gave him a look. Go crazy? That was what she did on the playing field. Not in art class. She wasn't even quite sure where to start.

It was even more frustrating to her because the rest of the students immediately started to paint. One girl sang to herself as she covered her canvas with bold strokes of blue and yellow. Another closed her eyes and simply let the paint fly. Astra stood in front of her blank canvas, uncharacteristically hesitant.

"Astra!" said the professor as he stepped up behind her. "Don't think, just do."

Astra put down her brush, turning to face him. "I'm just not creative," she told him, shaking her head. Then, catching his sympathetic look, she added hastily, "It doesn't bother me! I'm an athlete! I just don't have time to work on my creative side. No offense."

His eyes crinkled behind his round magenta glasses. "None taken, Starling," he said. "But we all have creativity inside of us. It's just that in some it is closer to the surface than others. We need to give ourselves permission to be open to it and then let ourselves go. No self-consciousness, no embarrassment. You must embrace it and then you'll really soar. Trust me, there's no other feeling quite like it."

Astra nodded and smiled agreeably, but when he moved on to the next student, she rolled her eyes. No other feeling like it? That was easy to say if you hadn't scored the winning basket in a tied game of star ball as the holo-clock was counting down, or broken a school record in the quarter-floozel dash. She couldn't imagine that spreading some paintlight on a holo-canvas could even come close to that feeling.

Having this enormous blank canvas in front of her was daunting. She felt unsure of herself, and that was unfamiliar and unpleasant. She dipped a large brush in her favorite color, bright red, which was sparkly.

"Don't think, just feel," the professor said in her ear. She hadn't realized he had returned, and his voice startled her. She jumped, her arm moved forward, and a big splash of shimmery red paintlight landed on the canvas.

"There you go," said Professor Claxworth encouragingly.

The red splatter might not have been intentional, but it did look good against the blank canvas. Encouraged,

Astra picked up another brush and coated it in sparkling yellow paintlight. She flicked the brush at the canvas, and splatters of sunshine covered the right side of the painting on top of the red. She started to feel bolder. Orange was next, then green, then purple. She decided she needed more red. She stepped back and took a look. The entire canvas was covered in overlapping strokes and splatters of paint. It was very bright and colorful. Cheerful, even. She tilted her head for another look. Then she frowned. Something was clearly missing.

"Nice work," said the professor, who had made his rounds and was back at Astra's side. He stared at the picture. "It's very pretty." He shook his head. "But I think it needs more of you in it."

Astra considered this. More of her? What exactly did that mean? She liked sports, action, movement. Maybe she should be more athletic in her approach to the canvas. She dipped her brush in orange paintlight, then jumped in the air, spun, and made a bold stroke on the canvas, layering on more color. That felt good! She did it again, this time with green. Even better. Then she had an idea. Was it crazy or was it brilliant? She'd find out in a moment. She looked around. Her professor was deep in conversation with a girl named Oola, who had covered her canvas with huge flower shapes in purple and pink. The other students were concentrating on their paintings. So no one saw Astra walk to the other side of the room and pour a large container of white paintlight over her head. She took a deep breath, ran across the room, did a flying leap and a double flip, and launched herself right at the painting. The springy canvas acted like a trampoline and she bounced back onto the floor, landing on her feet. She was now completely covered in paintlight—not just white, but every color of the rainbow. The rest of the students stared at her in shock.

Astra stood there, dripping. The colorful canvas now had a life-size Astra shape in the middle. She looked at it and grinned. It was totally strange, unique, and decidedly her.

Professor Findley Claxworth stood in the middle of the room in silence. Astra stared at him. Had she taken things too far?

"My heavens!" he finally exclaimed. "It's brilliant!" He turned to Astra. "What do you want to call it?"

"Um . . . *Athlete in Motion*?" she suggested, wiping paint from her eyebrows. She felt happy—exhilarated, even. Maybe there really was something to this creativity thing!

Oola gave her a look. "Um . . . you do know that if you leave paintlight on yourself for longer than twenty starmins, it totally stains, right?"

Astra turned to her professor. "Is that true?" she asked him. "It doesn't just disappear?"

He glanced down at his paintlight-splattered clothes, then at Astra. "Oh, yes!" he said. "Isn't it great? It is the one substance on Starland that will permanently stain fabric if you leave it on long enough."

"Um, then may I be excused to take a sparkle shower before next class?" Astra asked. As she spoke, she felt a drip slide down her cheek.

He looked starprised. "Well, certainly," he said. "But are you sure? I think you look great!"

Astra passed by a holo-trophy case and stole a glance at her paintlight-splattered reflection as she walked down the hallway. She was drenched! Still, she gave a little skip, then glanced around quickly to make sure no one had seen it. Maybe Aspirational Art wasn't so bad after all.

She was rounding the corner, heading toward the front door, when she heard Lady Stella's voice. She wasn't quite sure why, but she found herself ducking back into the shadows and pausing to listen. *Astra, what are you doing?* she thought. *Spying on the headmistress—what is wrong with you?* She peered around the corner. A woman wearing a dark cloak, the hood pulled over her head, was speaking earnestly with Lady Stella.

Astra holo-texted Piper:

 Hey! I'm out of class and outside Lady Stella's office. She's here. Do you think I should ask her if she's noticed what's been going on with everyone?

She pressed SEND.

The immediate response: HOLO-TEXT FAILURE.

"Thank you *mumble* for coming by. . . . I'm glad that you called the energy *mumble* to my attention. . . ." Astra's head jerked up. Had one of the women said the word *shortage*? But then again, it could have been *sport edge* or possibly even *report ledge*. She wasn't exactly sure. She strained to hear more, but the voices drifted into gibberish. Then she suddenly realized there were footfalls heading her way. She stepped forward and, most unfortunately, bumped right into the hooded woman. Some spy she was.

"Star apologies," said Astra, noticing that the woman's soft plum cloak was now streaked with white, purple, and red paintlight. "But you'll want to wash that in the next twenty starmins or it will be stained forever."

The woman stepped back when she saw Astra, and gathered her hood more tightly around her face. But not before Astra caught a glimpse of her delicate pointed chin and deep lavender eyes. She looked so familiar. Did Astra know her from somewhere? Perhaps she was an actress on holo-vison? "Star salutations," the woman said softly, and hurried down the hallway. Astra stared after her retreating back. Something about that woman seemed so familiar. . . .

But it wasn't coming to her.

She looked up. Lady Stella was standing in the doorway, watching her. "Star greetings, Astra," she said with a smile. "Looks like you had a good time in Aspirational Art class."

"I did," said Astra. "It was totally starprising, but I really did."

"It's about time," Lady Stella remarked. Astra shifted in her shiny red boots, feeling a bit uncomfortable that the headmistress knew she had been struggling with the class. Was Lady Stella keeping tabs on her? Maybe as a Star Darling she should have expected it. But it was still disconcerting.

"Who was that?" Astra asked the headmistress, pointing to the hooded woman, who was by then a small figure at the end of the long starmarble hallway.

"Oh, just someone . . . interviewing for a position," said Lady Stella vaguely.

"But she seemed so famil—" Astra said.

"So how have you been, Astra?" Lady Stella interrupted. Her piercing eyes, a kaleidoscope of colors, seemed to be staring right into her. Astra looked away.

"Okay," she replied. Should she bring up her concerns about the other Star Darlings? She desperately wanted to, but without Piper's input, she didn't feel like she should do it. So she changed the subject herself. "So what's going on with Ophelia?" she asked. "I heard she left Starling Academy. Kind of abruptly."

"Yes, sh-sh-sh-she did," said someone behind them. Lady Stella and Astra both spun around. Lady Cordial stood in the middle of the hallway, her purple hair escaping from her bun, and her cheeks flushed in an unbecoming shade of violet.

She caught her breath and continued. "We received some good news from the orphanage where Ophelia was from. They found a family who wanted to adopt her and sh-sh-she needed to return immediately to s-s-s-start the proceedings."

Lady Stella nodded. "Such wonderful news," she said.

So Cassie had been wrong. Ophelia *was* an orphan.

"Well, that's great," said Astra. "I'm really happy for her." She thought for a moment. "Maybe we could all send her a holo-card. Does she still have her Star-Zap?"

Lady Cordial shook her head.

"I guess we could send it to the orphanage," Astra said, pressing on. "What is it called?"

Lady Cordial frowned. "I think it was called the S-s-s-starland C-c-c-city Home for Orphaned S-s-s-star-ling Children."

Lady Stella shook her head. "Are you sure? I seem to recall it was called the Starland Memorial Institute."

"We'll let you know," said Lady Cordial. She stared at Astra. "Hadn't you better get back to your room to rinse off before the paintlight s-s-s-sets in and you're stained forever?"

Astra looked down. "Oh, that's right!" she said. With a quick farewell to the two faculty members, she hurried down the hall and to her dorm. She glanced at her Star-Zap and quickened her pace. She liked her aura red, not rainbow, thank you very much.

CHAPTER
3

Freshly sparkled and paintlight-free, Astra jumped onto the Cosmic Transporter, her starstick in hand. It was time for SD class and she didn't want to be late. She started to jog on the moving sidewalk, passing students who preferred a more leisurely ride, were upperclassmen with a free star period for their last class, or simply didn't care about their attendance records. She spotted a cluster of students chatting together on the transporter and, about to overtake them, shouted, "On your left!" so they would get out of her way. Suddenly, the floor stopped moving underneath her. The students she was about to pass all bumped into each other and began to fall like a bunch of stardominoes. To her great starprise, Astra found herself hurtling through the air, about to crash into the girls. Thinking quickly, she jammed her starstick down, lifted her body up, and vaulted right over them.

She landed neatly on her feet on the other side of the fallen girls. Brushing herself off, she stretched out her hand to the students, who had tumbled on top of each other in a very untidy pile.

"What happened?" a girl with shoulder-length bright yellow hair asked as Astra helped her to her feet.

"The Cosmic Transporter just stopped moving," said Astra. "How startacularly strange."

Once she had determined that the girls were not hurt, just shaken up, she headed to Star Darlings class.

The students, ensconced in the soundproof room they used for their private classes, were all chattering excitedly about the power outage. "The Cosmic Transporter just ground to a halt!" Astra informed them dramatically. "I'm lucky I didn't get hurt!"

"Nothing is working," said Piper. "It's like when the lights went out after Cassie's mission."

"Very strange," said Adora.

"What?" said Astra. She shook her head. Adora and her low talking! Adora opened her mouth to speak again.

"It's okay," said Astra. "Never mind."

The girls' Star-Zaps chimed and flickered. They all

had received a holo-message. Tessa read it first. "Oh, no, Professor Illumia Wickes is trapped in the Flash Vertical Mover!" she said. "No class today."

"Every cloud has a sparkly lining," said Scarlet, who then skipped right out the door. She almost knocked into Libby, who appeared in the doorway with a large bandage on her forehead.

"What happened?" asked Adora.

"What happened?" asked Astra.

Libby yawned, covering her mouth with her hand. "I was on the Cosmic Transporter on my way to class. The next thing I knew, I was under a pile of students!" She sat in her seat and put her head down on the desk.

Astra exchanged glances with Piper. They both realized that Libby must have fallen asleep standing up.

"Since we're all here—well, everyone but Scarlet, that is—I have some news to share," said Astra. "I ran into Lady Stella and Lady Cordial earlier today and they told me that Ophelia really *is* an orphan. And that she's getting adopted. That's why she left Starling Academy so abruptly. I'm just not sure which orphanage she is at," Astra continued. "Lady Cordial said it was called the Starland City Home for Orphaned Starling Children and Lady Stella thought it was Starland Memorial Institute."

She looked to Cassie for her reaction, but Cassie was too engrossed in posing for starselfies.

"So, Cassie," she said loudly, "it looks like your theory was totally wrong."

Cassie put down her Star-Zap for a moment and smiled distractedly. "Yes, I do have many theories," she said. "In fact, I shared seventeen of them today in my classes. Everyone was very impressed, I could tell."

"Really," said Astra. "Seventeen, you say."

"Really," said Cassie. "I have a fascinating way of looking at things, and I enjoy sharing my perspective with my fellow students."

Vega spoke up. "Now this may truly sound absurd," she said. "But should we take Lady Stella's word?"

Astra paused, digesting Vega's rhyme. "So you think she isn't telling the truth?" she finally said.

"The answer is I'm just not sure," Vega replied. "But maybe we should find out more."

"That's a good point," said Astra. "I'll try to get in touch with the orphanage and verify that information."

Piper nodded. "Good plan."

"Well, I'm going to call the orphanage right this very starmin," said Leona. She walked across the room and proceeded to photobomb Cassie's starselfies. Astra sighed and looked around the room. Adora was moving her lips, but no sound came out. Libby snored gently, her head resting on her desk. Vega opened her mouth to speak. Piper, seeing this, put her hands over her ears.

Astra had reached her limit. Enough was enough. "That's it!" she shouted. Everyone stopped talking and stared at her.

"Something really strange is going on, and none of you can see it," she said. "And it's driving me and Piper crazy!"

Tessa stared at Astra. "Maybe you two actually *are* crazy," she said, "if none of us can see it but you."

Astra looked around wildly, then noticed that Vega was holo-vidding her. "Vega, give that to me," she said brusquely. Vega scowled and opened her mouth, about to retort. "Please," Astra added. "I just want to look at some of your holo-vids." You never knew when Vega was going to start holo-vidding. Luckily, once Astra said the magic word, Vega handed it over without rhyming.

Astra began to quickly scan through the holo-vids. She found what she was looking for—breakfast that morning—and pressed the projector option. The cafeteria scene sprang to life in the middle of the room.

"Do you really think this is going to work?" whispered Piper.

Astra shrugged. "It's worth a try," she said.

Slowly, the Star Darlings began to drift over and watch. After a couple of moments, Cassie's mouth fell open in shock. Leona shook her head. "Oh, my stars," said Sage. She giggled, looked mortified, and slapped her hand over her mouth. Adora said something; no one knew what. Only Libby, still snoozing, did not react.

"Moonberries," whispered Tessa.

"Did I really just . . . skip?" asked someone in a horrified-sounding voice.

Astra spun around. Scarlet was standing in the open doorway.

"I forgot my Star-Zap," she explained. "Is that holo-vid for real?"

Astra nodded grimly. "It's for real."

"Well, then we have to do something about this!" Scarlet said, her cheeks bright pink with embarrassment. "Right now!"

Vega nodded. She opened her mouth, then shut it. It was clear that she didn't want to talk because she knew she would start rhyming again. Finally, with a look of resignation on her face, she said, "I thought that you were being cruel. But I really am a rhyming fool."

CHAPTER
4

Now that everyone was aware of their strange behavior, they wanted it fixed, and fast. The problem was that nobody had any idea how to fix it.

Later that night, after they had attended their various meetings and clubs and had an unusually quiet dinner, the girls gathered in Astra and Clover's room, where they could talk freely.

After everyone was settled on couches, chairs, and the floor, Astra started the conversation. "I know it was kind of shocking to watch Vega's holo-vid today and be able to see how you all have been acting. Piper and I think the key to finding out why it is happening has to do with the fact that the two of us are acting normally."

Leona snorted.

"Very funny, Leona," said Astra. She smiled. "Well, acting as normally as we usually act, anyway."

Adora typed into her Star-Zap and passed it to Piper, who sat next to her. This had become her new way of communicating since she had been informed that her voice was inaudible. CLEARLY IT WAS YOUR TRIP TO WISHWORLD, she'd written.

Piper considered this and shook her head. "Oh, I don't think so," she said.

"Yeah, I'm pretty sure that's just a coincidence," Astra informed her.

"What makes you think that?" asked Gemma.

"Because Piper and I never acted odd, even before we went to Wishworld," Astra explained. "So it must be something else."

Piper nodded in agreement, but the only response from the other Star Darlings was laughter. And it wasn't just from Sage.

"What's going on?" Astra asked, feeling irritated.

Vega looked up from her Star-Zap guiltily. "I found a holo-vid of you. You will not like it, this is true." She held up her Star-Zap and projected the image. It was of the Star Darlings sitting around their table in the Celestial Café a starweek earlier, eating lunch. Astra and

Piper watched in disbelief as Piper finished everyone's sentences, sometimes quite incorrectly, and Astra pulled one silly practical joke after another—pulling out a chair as Scarlet was about to sit down, switching Gemma's iced Zing with Tessa's ozziefruit juice, gluing a fork to the table . . .

"Ohhhhh," said Astra, feeling completely mortified. Piper blushed and looked at the floor.

"So since you two were acting odd *before* the mission and then stopped once you got back, clearly something happened on the trip to reverse it," said Tessa.

"Maybe it has something to do with traveling through the atmosphere?" suggested Clover.

Astra frowned. "I don't think that's it," she said. She began to pace the room, thinking.

"Did you do anything out of the ordinary on Wishworld?" asked Gemma.

Tessa perked up. "Did you eat something different?" she suggested.

"Oh! Maybe it was the chocolate egg creams!" Piper said.

"What's that?" Tessa wanted to know.

"A delicious Wishling concoction of seltzer, chocolate syrup, and milk!" Piper explained. "We each drank one."

"That must be it!" said Tessa, licking her lips. "How do we get one?"

Astra was not convinced. "I just don't think that's it," she said. "But what could it be?" Absentmindedly, she put her hands on the ground and flipped her legs into the air. There! That was much better. She did her best thinking upside down; she was sure of it. As she roamed the room, walking on her hands, she saw Cassie's silver slippers, Clover's purple boots, and the star ball she had been looking for for a double starweek. Then she spotted a pair of bare feet, the toes sinking into the thick carpet. They had to belong to Piper, who often remarked that walking barefoot helped her relax. Astra noticed that Piper's toenails were a deep sparkly blue, which reminded her of her mission and the slumber party they had attended, where they had given each other . . .

Astra toppled over. "That's it!" she said from the floor. She was so excited she couldn't even wait until she stood up to speak. "It's the nail polish! Piper and I went to a sleepover and everyone gave each other manicures and pedicures. We had to take off our Starland polish first. And then, when we got back home, we could see that the rest of you were acting odd. All we have to do is remove your polish, and everything will be back to normal!"

The Star Darlings headed straight to the starbeauty-chambers in the Lightning Lounge where they had put on the polish in the first place. They eagerly sat down and accessed the polish removal function. But when their hands emerged from the pods, the polish was as shiny and perfect as ever. Adora tried over and over, to no avail.

"It's no use, Adora," Cassie told her.

"I can't believe none of you can hear me!" Adora said.

Cassie nodded. "You're right, this color does look great on me," she said. "But pretty as it is, we've still got to figure out how to remove it." She looked around at the group. "Moons and stars," she said. "Was I just bragging again?"

They next tried to scrape it off with the scratchiest materials they could find—leaves from the ruffruff tree, pieces of eternium wool, and prickly buds—but nothing worked. Adora ran off to her room and returned with vanisholine, which smelled so terrible the girls down the hall came by to complain, but it didn't make a dent in the polish. As a last resort, they tried to scrape it off with Sage's crystal from the Crystal Mountains, the hardest substance on Starland, but even that didn't work. The nail polish was impervious to everything. The girls stared at their colorful nails in disbelief.

"So how did you get yours off?" Leona finally asked.

"With this magical Wishworld potion that they use at slumber parties," said Piper.

"That's right," said Astra. "It's called the polish of removal. Whoever goes down to Wishworld next has to bring this magic elixir back with them. Apparently it's the only way to take this crazy polish off."

"I am furious!" Leona said. "So we have to wait, knowing we're acting like weirdos, and there's nothing we can do about it." She saw everyone staring at her. "I'm smiling, aren't I?" she asked.

Astra sighed. She hoped someone would get sent down to Wishworld and fast, to collect wish energy and also to bring back the magical polish of removal. Because now not only was everyone still doing the weird stuff, but they were annoyed with themselves for not being able to stop doing it.

After everyone had left for their rooms, looking disappointed, and Clover had hugged her tightly before heading off to take a sparkle shower, apologizing as she did so, Astra picked up her Star-Zap. In all the excitement, she had completely forgotten to call the orphanage! She was eager to verify that Lady Stella was correct. There was enough going on without the Star Darlings distrusting their leader, too.

Astra flipped open her Star-Zap. "Give me the numbers of all the orphanages in Starland City," she said. It turned out there was just one.

A pleasant-looking woman with turquoise hair in a neat bun answered the call. "Starland City Home for Orphaned Starling Children," she said. "Star greetings. How may I help you?"

"I wanted to verify the name of one of your, um . . . orphans," Astra said awkwardly. "Her name is—"

"I'm sorry," the woman interrupted. "Our students' privacy is very strictly maintained. We don't give out information about anyone over a communication device. If you want to request information on someone here, you must come in person."

"How about I say her name and you nod if she's there?" Astra suggested—rather cunningly, she thought. "Her name is O—"

The woman shook her head emphatically. "I'm sorry, but that is against the rules. Good night." The screen went black.

Astra scowled, then consulted her star schedule. Her Chronicle Class professor was out, so she had third and fourth periods free the next day. If she hurried, that was probably enough time to take a quick trip into Starland City. She holo-texted Piper:

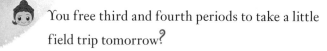

You free third and fourth periods to take a little field trip tomorrow?

Sure. I've got study hall, and Professor Roberta Elsa never takes attendance.

Astra smiled. Piper didn't ask questions; she knew that if Astra asked, it must be important. Astra's Star-Zap beeped and she realized that a holo-message had come in while she had been talking to the unhelpful orphanage lady. She glanced down and saw that it was a holo-card from her family. She opened it. Instantly, her mom, dad, and two younger siblings appeared in a small 3-D holographic image, which beamed into the air in front of her. They sat around the dinner table, one chair noticeably empty. She could even smell the food they were having— flug and beans, her favorite.

Everyone immediately began talking over each other, as they always did.

"Hope you are having fun at Starling Academy!" her mom said tearfully.

"I'm redecorating our room!" shouted her little sister, Asia. Their dad gave her a look. "Well, I'm trying to convince Mom and Dad, anyway," she said. "More stuffed animals, fewer holo-trophies."

"She's kidding, Astra," her mom hurriedly interjected. "Your trophies and medals aren't going anywhere!"

"We miss you!" they shouted, waving at her.

Ajax threw a napkin at the camera. And then they were gone.

Astra smiled. Her nice, normal, boring family. They didn't quite understand Astra and her relentless quest for greatness both on the field and off. Maybe someday they would.

Directly after second period, Astra headed for the hover bus stop, right outside the main entrance to Starling Academy. She stood under the canopy of kaleidoscope trees, the blooms slowly shifting from bright orange to sunny yellow above her head. She pulled out her Star-Zap and accessed the bus schedule. It would be arriving in a starmin and a half. Where was Piper? Just then, she heard footfalls and looked up to see her rushing across the street. Or Piper's version of rushing, which to anyone else looked like a leisurely stroll. Her seafoam hair fluttered around her shoulders, and she was wearing a long flowing dress, as usual, plus a floppy hat. It wasn't a look Astra thought she could pull off—not that she particularly wanted to, mind you—but it seemed right on Piper.

As the bus appeared in the distance, Astra filled Piper in. "We're going to the orphanage to locate Ophelia," she said, "and confirm the story. If all goes as planned, we'll be back in time for fifth period."

"Good," said Piper. "We wouldn't want to miss Color Catching."

The hover bus pulled up silently and the side lifted to let them in, revealing Starlings relaxing in comfortable chaises. The two girls stepped on board and settled into their seats. A Bot-Bot conductor zoomed up to register their destination and collect their payment. They flashed their Star-Zaps. "You will reach your destination in eleven starmins," the Bot-Bot said. "Have a pleasant ride."

The bus had two rows of seats on either side, separated by an aisle. All the seats faced the windows so the riders could enjoy the scenery. Piper took off her hat, placed it on the seat next to her, and turned to Astra. "I'm actually looking forward to seeing Ophelia," she said. "She may have been a terrible Star Darling but she really is a sweet girl."

"Yeah," said Astra. "She is. It will be nice to see her, see how she's doing." She thought for a moment. "I really hope the news about her adoption is true." *For Ophelia's sake as well as Lady Stella's,* she thought.

Piper didn't answer. Astra looked at her. She had started meditating, sitting cross-legged with her hands, palms up, on her knees. Astra looked around at her fellow passengers: an elderly lady, cyber-knitting what looked like the world's longest scarf; a woman napping in the sunlight; two parents with a baby; and a boy, about Astra's age, engrossed in a holo-book. His hair was deep indigo and his skin a sparkly golden brown. He was wearing a school uniform, possibly from Star Preparatory, the all-boys school across Luminous Lake. Just then, to her dismay, he looked up, and their eyes met. He smiled at Astra, and she realized that her face was inexplicably getting warm. *What is wrong with you, Astra?* she thought. Her life, until that very moment, had been completely focused on sports, school, and, recently, the Star Darlings. Boys had never been a consideration; she simply didn't have the time or the interest.

She looked away quickly and faced forward, staring out at the scenery. The rural surroundings of the Starling Academy campus gave way to suburban houses with big lawns and then to city blocks tightly packed with stores and apartment buildings. The number of people—and vehicles—increased dramatically.

What was she supposed to be focusing on? Oh, yes—Ophelia. Astra had bigger things to think about than boys from across the lake. Even very cute boys from across the lake. She snuck another look at him and immediately looked away. He was looking right back at her, a broad smile on his face.

"He's cute," said Piper, her eyes still closed.

"Piper!" said Astra. "What are you talking about? You didn't even look."

"I can just tell," she said with a secret smile.

Piper could be spooky that way sometimes. "Whatever," said Astra irritably. "Our stop is coming up."

The Bot-Bot conductor zoomed over. "Your destination is approaching," it confirmed.

The bus rolled to a stop on a busy street corner and the door slid up. The two girls disembarked and consulted their Star-Zaps for directions.

"Excuse me," someone said. Astra and Piper turned around. Moons and stars! It was the boy from the hover bus.

"You left this behind," he said, holding out Piper's hat.

"Star salutations!" said Piper. "How kind of you. I hope you didn't have to get off the bus early."

"Oh, it's okay," he said gallantly. "I only had a few more stops to go. I'm going to the Abramowicz Center to check out their interactive holo-exhibit on wish energy kineticism." He suddenly looked bashful. "Besides . . . I wanted to introduce myself."

Oh, he wanted to meet *Piper*. Astra felt a rush of disappointment.

He turned to her. "You're Astra, right?" he asked.

She started. "Yes! How did you know?"

He gave her a big grin. "I'm a huge star ball fan and you're one of the best players on Starland, that's how. I follow your stats. They're totally startacular," he said. "My name is Leebeau," he added.

"Nice to meet you, Leebeau," said Astra. "This is Piper, by the way."

Piper and Leebeau exchanged pleasantries. Then Leebeau turned back to Astra.

"Well, see you around," he said. He waved to them both and was on his way.

"Well, he *was* pretty cute," said Piper. "And he certainly has a crush on you, that's for sure."

"Shut your stars," said Astra quickly. But she was secretly pleased.

The two girls walked a couple of blocks to the orphanage and were soon standing in front of a building from a bygone era, made entirely of glimmering star-marble and complete with intricate holo-glass windows in brilliant colors. "They don't make them like they used to," Piper remarked. It was such an old lady thing to say that Astra laughed. Piper gave her a look. "What's so funny?" she asked.

At the top of the steep stairs was another old-fashioned touch—a wish energy bell pull. Astra concentrated on ringing it, and after a while, when she got the hang of it, the door slid open. They stepped inside a dark yet cheerful room. It was comfortable and cozy, with a large rug of old Starlandian design in the middle of the floor, overstuffed armchairs, and colorful pillows. On the walls were holo-photos of smiling kids and shelves full of holo-books.

The receptionist, whom Astra had spoken to the day before, sat in front of a holo-screen, typing away on a holo-keyboard.

"Star apologies," she said. "I'm under a deadline and need to file this report immediately. I'll be with you in a starmin."

Piper grew more anxious and Astra more agitated as a quarter starhour ticked by. Worriedly, Piper checked her Star-Zap. Third period was over and fourth was about to begin. Piper shifted nervously in her seat.

"Um, are you almost done?" Astra asked the woman.

"Almost," she replied distractedly as she frowned at the screen and began rearranging her text with a few carefully placed swipes.

"There," said the woman as she typed the final line and pressed SEND. She turned to the girls. "Star greetings," she said. "Star apologies for the delay. How can I help you?"

"We're here from Starling Academy," Astra said. "We need to talk to a student named Ophelia."

"Oh, Starling Academy!" said the woman, appearing impressed. She took a closer look at Astra. "You look familiar. Did you holo-call yesterday?"

"I did," said Astra. "You told me to come in person, so here we are."

The woman's turquoise bun bobbed as she accessed the student schedules. "Ophelia is in Moonematics class right now. Let me see if she can be interrupted." She stood up and walked to a tall doorway. She paused before opening it. "Who should I say is here to see her?" she asked.

"Astra and Piper," Astra said.

"Astra and Piper from Starling Academy," said the receptionist. "I'll be right back."

Several starmins later the door slid open and the woman stepped back into the room. The door shut behind her. She was frowning. "I found Ophelia, but she says she doesn't know you, or anyone from Starling Academy."

"No," said Astra stubbornly. "She definitely knows us. If we could just see her for one starmin . . ."

The door began to slide open again behind the receptionist. Astra caught a quick glimpse of overalls and sneakers.

"Ophelia!" Astra said.

The door fully opened. There stood a girl of medium height with bright pink hair.

"You're not Ophelia," said Astra.

"I most certainly am," said the girl with a laugh. "I'm just not *your* Ophelia."

"Star apologies," said Piper quickly.

"Not necessary," said the girl. "Can I get back to class?" she asked the receptionist. "We're in the middle of discussing infinite integers."

"Of course," said the woman. She turned to Astra and Piper. "I'm afraid that she's the only Ophelia in the whole place."

Piper pulled out her Star-Zap. "Can you just take a quick look at her holo-photo?" she said. She projected a picture of Ophelia, taken during a game of Poses they had played one evening after dinner. Ophelia was balancing on one leg, looking sweetly serious. Astra could be seen in the background in the middle of one of her famous up-and-over starflips.

The woman peered at the holo-photo and shook her head. "No, she doesn't look familiar at all," she said. "Star apologies, Starlings. I wish I could have been of help."

Astra and Piper headed down the front steps dejectedly. "Maybe she's lying," Astra muttered.

Piper gave her a quizzical look. "What reason would she have to lie?" she asked. "Somebody is lying, that's for sure. And her name is Ophelia."

CHAPTER
5

As they trudged back to the bus stop, Astra tried to look on the bright side of things. "Well, at least we'll be back in time for Color Catching cla—" She broke off as their Star-Zaps began to chime and flicker.

SD WISH ORB IDENTIFIED. PROCEED TO LADY STELLA'S OFFICE IMMEDIATELY.

"Moons and stars!" Astra and Piper exclaimed at the same time. But they didn't laugh; they were too panicked. They were going to be late for the Wish Orb reveal! That had never happened before, and this was the one event Astra did not want to come first in.

"Let's go!" said Astra. The two girls raced down the street, Astra accessing the holo–bus schedule as she ran. "We might just make it if we hurry!" she shouted. She rounded the corner to see the bus sitting at the stop. "It's still here!" she shouted, and put on a burst of speed, reasoning that she could hold the bus for her slower friend. But even with her stellar track skills, by the time she arrived at the stop, the bus was gone.

"*Oh, starf!*" she yelled, stamping her foot. "There isn't another hover bus for fifteen starmins," she told Piper, once the girl had caught up. "We're never going to make it."

Piper peered down the street. "Hey!" she shouted. "It looks like the hover bus is stopping up ahead!"

"Startacular!" said Astra.

The two girls hurried. The door lifted up and they clambered on, Piper completely out of breath.

"Thank you," Astra said to the Bot-Bot conductor.

"Don't thank me. Thank him," said the Bot-Bot. "He's the one who saw you."

What in the stars? Astra turned around and there he was—Leebeau, a sunny grin on his sparkly face.

"Fancy seeing you two again," he said.

Neither girl was able to respond: Piper because she was panting so hard, unaccustomed as she was to quarter-floozel dashes or running up and down a star ball field; Astra because she was overwhelmed by the overpowering and unfamiliar feeling in the pit of her stomach. It was like she was going down the biggest drop on a giant star coaster. Wearing a blindfold.

What was going on?

"How was your trip?" Leebeau asked as they all took their seats.

"Okay," Astra managed to squeak out at the same time Piper caught her breath and answered, "Not so good."

"You've got to get your stories straight," he said with a laugh. "In any event, I bet it was better than mine. Turns out the Abramowicz Center is closed today. That's what I get for not checking first."

Astra nodded, glancing down at her Star-Zap anxiously.

"Are you late for class or something?" he asked her.

Astra nodded. "Or something," she said.

Leebeau got a mischevious twinkle in his eye. "Listen, I know just the thing. Since we're the only ones on this bus, I'm going to let you in on a little trick. We can access the hyper-speed function on this bus with a few swipes on my communicator."

"Are you sure it's safe?" asked Piper.

"I'm positive," he said.

"Do it!" said Astra.

Leebeau flipped open his communicator, swiped a

few times, and—*whoosh!*—they were in front of the black curlicued gates of Starling Academy. The Bot-Bot conductor raced down the aisle, its eyes flashing in alarm. "This is highly unusual!" it said.

The door lifted and Astra stood and turned to Leebeau, a happy smile on her face. "Star salutations!" she cried. "We owe you one!"

"Just wave to me at your next game," he said. He made a fist and pumped it in the air. "Go, Glowin' Glions!"

The two girls waved good-bye and hurried through the campus gates.

Piper spoke first. "If I didn't know any better, I'd think that maybe you were starting to have a crush on Leboy," she said.

"Leebeau!" Astra said, correcting her.

"I knew it!" said Piper with satisfaction.

"You don't know anything," said Astra dismissively. But the truth was that *she* was the one who didn't know what was going on. Luckily, she had the Wish Orb reveal to concentrate on instead.

"Thank the stars you're here!" said Lady Stella as Astra and Piper burst into her office moments later. "We were starting to worry!" Everyone was seated around the silver table in the middle of the headmistress's cavernous office. Astra and Piper silently slipped into the two empty seats.

Leona leaned over and whispered in Astra's ear. "Where were you guys?"

"I'll tell you later," Astra whispered back. Now that she was seated, she started to feel the buzz of excitement. With all the strange things going on, she hadn't focused on the fact that the next mission could actually finally be hers. She counted in her head. Sage, Libby, Leona, Vega, Ophelia—make that Scarlet—Cassie, and Piper had all gone on their missions already. That left her, Tessa, Gemma, Clover, and Adora. The odds were in her favor. And she was ready to go.

On her right side sat Libby. It looked like her eyelids were getting heavy. Astra poked her in the side, perhaps a bit too roughly.

"Mom, I told you, I'm awake!" Libby shouted. Then she looked around at everyone at the table, embarrassed. "My stars, was I drifting off again?" she asked. Astra nodded.

Gemma looked around the room. "No Wish Cavern this time?" she asked.

"No, the Wish Orb has something else in mind

today," said Lady Stella. She was suddenly holding a tray with five golden cups on it. Astra blinked. That tray had not been anywhere in sight a starsec ago; she was sure of it.

"The five remaining Starlings who have not yet gone on their missions—and I'm certain you all know who you are—need to keep their eye on the cups as they move about the table," Lady Stella said, smiling at the group. "One by one you will have a chance to select a cup and lift it. The Star Darling who is intended to go on this mission will be the one to find the orb."

Well, that was different. As Lady Stella placed the golden cups on the table, Astra's fingers moved involuntarily, eager to choose.

Before their amazed eyes, the golden cups began to slide around the table, moved by an unseen force. They flew by, faster and faster, until they were just a blur. Finally, they came to a stop in the middle of the table. Five identical golden cups. Which one could be hiding the orb?

Tessa went first. She stood up, took a deep breath, reached across the table for one cup, changed her mind, and placed her hands on another. She lifted it, letting her breath out all in a rush. Nothing.

"Moonberries!" she said in disgust. That this was her

new expletive would have made Astra laugh out loud, but she was too keyed up at the moment to crack a smile.

"Now it's your turn, Adora," said Lady Stella.

"Star salutations," said Adora.

"Excuse me?" said Lady Stella.

Adora shook her head as if to say that it didn't matter. She then placed her hands on the cup directly in front of her and closed her eyes. She picked up the cup and opened them. Astra couldn't hear her, but she could clearly read her lips. "Starf!" Adora said. Actually, thought Astra, it was a good thing it wasn't Adora's turn to go to Wishworld. Her Wisher would not have been able to hear a thing she said! Adora flipped the cup to peer inside, as if to see if the orb was hiding from her, playing tricks.

"Your turn," Lady Stella said to Astra.

And suddenly, Astra knew exactly which cup to lift. She reached over and placed her hand on top of it.

"No!" said Leona. "Tessa already picked that one!" But Astra shook her head. She knew she was right, the same as she knew that you never, ever threw a lolopitch when the runner was on her first leg in starshoot and that you always bobbled in the final three starsecs of a tenth. She smiled at Lady Stella and lifted the cup off the table.

"Ohhhhhh!" breathed the Star Darlings. For under the cup a brilliant orb was floating in midair, looking exactly like a miniature star ball. Astra tossed it into the air and cradled it in her hands. "It's mine, it's finally mine," she said.

"The Wish Orb has chosen," Lady Stella pronounced. "Starkudos, Astra."

A blur of activity followed. Once everyone had left, congratulating Astra (though she could tell that four Star Darlings—Adora, Tessa, Gemma, and Clover—were perhaps not as pleased for her as the others, and who could blame them?), she met with Lady Stella and received her instructions, then got a briefing on shooting star travel and the trip to Wishworld, an upgrade to her Star-Zap, and a quick lesson on the Wishworld Outfit Selector.

When she left the headmistress's office, she let out a sigh of relief. There had been no inquiry into why she and Piper had been late, for which she was very grateful. Until she knew for sure what was going on, she didn't want to make any accusations or show her hand. However, as she had stared into the brilliant kaleidoscope eyes of her headmistress, Astra couldn't help wondering: *Is she who she says she is?* Truth be told, she was finding it almost impossible to believe that Lady Stella could be anything but a stellarly trustworthy leader, but there was still a small glimmer of doubt she couldn't shake.

The meeting ran late, so by the time she made it to the Celestial Café, there was just time for a quick star sandwich. She wolfed it down and headed to her room. She would leave for Wishworld early the next morning. The rest of the evening was hers.

Astra bounded into her room to find her room-mate, Clover, sitting cross-legged on her bed, playing her keyboard and jotting down lyrics. "Astra!" she said delightedly. Clearly she had gotten over her disappoint-ment at not being chosen. Astra could see that the girl was struggling not to stand up and rush over to her. Astra was feeling generous. "That's okay," she said. "Get over here." She held her arms open.

"Sorry," Clover said into Astra's hair as she squeezed her tightly for a moment. She broke the hug and stood back, staring at her.

"This is so exciting, Astra," she said.

Astra couldn't contain herself. "It is!" she shouted. She hopped onto her bed and started jumping up and down.

"No flips!" said Clover in a warning tone. "Remember

what happened last time? You almost flew right out the window!"

"All right, all right," said Astra. She dropped to the bed and bounced a few times.

"So let me see your Star-Zap!" said Clover excitedly. "Should we flip through some Wishworld fashions? Cassie told me that's what she and Sage did the night before their missions."

Astra looked down at her clothes. She dressed sporty. Very sporty. Hair pulled back, knee-length shorts, a T-shirt, tube socks, and sneakers. "Do I look like I want to make a fashion statement?" she asked her roommate.

Clover, who picked out her own outfits with great care, looked disappointed.

"So what do you think the wish will be?" she asked, changing the subject.

Astra reached her arms above her head and stretched. "I don't know," she said. "I'm hoping it has to do with sports, or some kind of competition."

Clover nodded. "That would make sense," she said. She thought for a minute. "But will it be confusing, since Wishworld sports are so different from ours?"

Astra shrugged. "How different could they be?" she asked. "From what I've seen of Wishworld sports from the Wishworld Surveillance Deck, the movements are all the same—throwing, hitting, tagging, kicking, catching, flipping, leaping, jumping, tumbling, sliding, tackling. It's just the rules that are different. That's easy enough to figure out."

"I'm dying to see how the Cyber Journal works," Clover said. "Can you make a mental observation?"

Astra considered this and smiled. "Well, we're only supposed to use it on Wishworld, but I guess once won't hurt," she said. She accessed her Cyber Journal, pushed the record button, handed Clover the Star-Zap, and made her observation.

And before Clover's amazed eyes appeared: *Star Observation: Note to self, get new roommate.*

"Oh, Astra!" said Clover with a laugh. She threw a small star-shaped pillow at her roommate and it bounced off Astra's head.

"They don't call it a *throw* pillow for nothing," joked Astra.

Clover began getting ready for bed, but Astra found she was still full of excited energy. She headed to the Radiant Recreation Center and went for a run on the startrack, which helped relax her a bit. Then she returned to her dorm room and, in the dim light so as not to wake up her already-sleeping roommate, put on pajamas, slipped on her headphones so she could absorb her lessons, and finally fell into a deep sleep. In her dreams she played strange sports with unfamiliar equipment in a vast arena, and despite her confusion, she was presented with a medal in front of a roaring crowd—which happened to include a handsome boy with indigo hair and golden-brown skin. She didn't need Piper to interpret that dream. Clearly her subconscious was telling her that her mission was going to be a success. She just wasn't sure why Leebeau had been there. Why was she dreaming about someone she hadn't even known existed that morning at breakfast? That was startastically odd indeed.

"Good-bye, Astra!"

"Good luck!"

"Safe star travels!"

The Star Darlings were all clustered around Astra, getting a little too close for her personal comfort. "Back up, guys!" she said, waving them away. Still, it was nice that they were so excited for her. Piper pushed to the front and spoke softly. "I'll keep looking for Ophelia while you're gone," she said. "Do you think I should ask Leona for help? I know she was worried about her."

"That's a great idea," said Astra. "See if there's anything you two can find out." She paused. "But don't forget that she's going to say one thing and do the opposite. It could get confusing."

"I'll remember," said Piper.

Sage squeezed Astra's hand. "Think things through, try not to draw too much attention to yourself, and be careful," she said with a laugh. "I'll be sending you good thoughts."

Astra got an unexpected lump in her throat. She and Sage could be real competitors, so that meant a lot to her. "Star salutations, Sage," she said.

Tessa leaned in next and gave her a hug. "Can't argue with the Wish Orb," she said. "This one is all yours. Good luck to you."

Adora was the last Star Darling to see her off. "The best of luck, Astra," she said sincerely. "And just keep in mind that we're here for you if you need us."

"Huh?" said Astra. "I mean . . . uh, thanks!"

A star had been captured. The wranglers would only be able to hold on to it for so long and it was time for Astra to go. Lady Cordial handed Astra a red backpack with a star on it. Lady Stella turned to Astra. "I would wish you luck, but I don't think you need it. You are bold and strong and full of confidence. Never lose that."

She paused. "But you must also remember that there is strength in vulnerability, as well."

"There is?" asked Astra.

"There is," Lady Stella said.

Astra had had enough advice. She was done with good-byes. She motioned for the Star Wranglers to help her onto her star and release it, and she shot off into the ether. It was time to start her mission!

CHAPTER
6

After her relatively boring trip down to Wishworld to help Piper with her mission, Astra was hoping for a wilder ride this time. Sure, there were some bumps along the way and some stomach-scrambling spins, and she did narrowly avoid hitting an asteroid, but all in all it was a disappointment, in her opinion.

COMMENCE APPEARANCE CHANGE, her Star-Zap announced. Astra accessed her Wishworld Outfit Selector and put on a sporty yet sassy outfit. It wasn't very different from her Starland apparel, just a lot less sparkly. It was her signature style and practical, too, as you never knew when you'd have to sub in for someone on the playing field (or so Astra hoped).

Now it was time to make sure her skin and hair lost

their Starland sparkle, too. She began to recite: "Star light, star bright, the first star I see tonight: I wish I may, I wish I might, have the wish I wish tonight." She watched with amazement as her skin lost its glimmer, and from the corner of her eye she could see that her hair was no longer bright red but a dark reddish brown. Since clothes and hair and accessories were not her thing, she really did not mind at all.

APPROACHING WISHWORLD ATMOSPHERE, said the Star-Zap. That's when things livened up a little, as the star began to buck and bump.

"Whee!" yelled Astra with glee. But all too soon the ride was smooth again.

She was hoping the landing might be exciting, but it was completely uneventful, to her disappointment. She touched down gently in a stand of trees, well hidden from curious eyes. Astra stood and stretched her legs. She was pleased to note that the air was warm and the sun was shining. It was a beautiful Wishworld day. She waited patiently as the star finished sparking, then picked it up and folded it down to pocket size. She accessed the directions to Pine Brook School, where she would find her Wisher, and set off at a quick pace in a northwest direction.

But there was so much to see along the way! Astra's

last visit to Wishworld had been centered in a limited area in a small town, and she now found herself in a park, which was of much more interest to her. She passed a small body of water and admired some swimming creatures. She was shocked when one of them suddenly unfolded its wings, started flapping them, and then lifted itself out of the water and began to soar through the air! They made funny noises that she tried to copy. "Quack!" she cried, and she was pretty sure they quacked right back at her. She heard some chirpy whistling and looked up to find adorable feathered creatures hopping from branch to branch. The many trees were all shades of one color—green—but they were attractive nonetheless.

She had to tear herself away but finally headed out of the park and made her way to a busy road. She walked alongside it on a grassy embankment as the cars passed by. Next she came to a fenced-in field. A man was blowing a whistle and kids were running around kicking a black-and-white patterned ball. So Astra, even though she knew she should be hurrying along, had to rest her arms on the fence and watch. The game reminded her a lot of star ball—without the wish energy, of course—and, she realized, in this game you could only use your feet. Each team had to direct the ball to the other team's net, which was guarded by a player who, oddly enough, *could* use her hands. If it got past that player, the other team scored a throw, which there on Wishworld was quite obviously called a "gooooaaaal!" The game looked like a lot of fun (even without the use of wish energy), and she wished she could join in. That she was twice the height of any of the players kept her on the sidelines.

The whistle sounded. "Game is over!" the man shouted. "Time to get back to class!"

Starf! It was time for Astra to get to class, too. She glanced down at her Countdown Clock. She had wasted more than one of her precious Wishworld hours and she hadn't even arrived at her Wisher's school yet! *Correction*, she told herself. She hadn't wasted the time at all. She was observing Wishworld life. She hadn't recorded a single observation, though. She should get started on that.

I wish I was already at my Wisher's school, she thought. *WHOOSH!* There was an unexpected blast of air, a moment of blurry discombobulation, and as soon as Astra caught her breath she realized she was standing right in front of Clarkston Mills School. *My stars!* thought Astra. *My talent must be teleporting.* A woman with short dark hair and piercing blue eyes sat behind a desk.

"May I help you?" the woman asked.

"My name is Astra," she said, as she had been instructed. "I am a new student in school."

"Your name is Astra. You are a new student in school." The woman frowned and leaned forward. "You do know that this is the next-to-last week of school, don't you? Kind of an odd time to start!"

"Well, better late than never!" said Astra brightly.

Then the woman's expression changed as she sniffed the air. "Why, I do believe that is devil's food cake." She sniffed again. "With fudge frosting, if I'm not mistaken." Her eyes misted over. "My grandfather was a baker and I used to help him after school. That was my favorite cake of them all. I'll have to go to the cafeteria and get a slice later." She smiled. "Come right in, Astra. Do you know which classroom to go to?"

"I'll find my way," Astra told her.

The woman nodded. "You'll find your way."

Astra followed the directions her Star-Zap provided and was soon pushing open a set of double doors. She was back outside again, to her delight. And she was treated to a most welcoming sight. Dozens of Wishlings, all milling about, playing games in the sunshine. Was it P.E. class or a non-compulsory-between-class recreational break like they had on Starland? Not that it really mattered. There was a group of kids hitting a round white ball back and forth over a net. Some were kicking around the same type of black-and-white ball she had seen earlier. Others were bouncing a brown ball on the ground and taking turns tossing it into a net high above their heads. When they got it in, they slapped hands.

She loped over to that group, and without a second thought, she ran into the middle of the game and grabbed the ball. It was different from a star ball—larger, more solid—and it had a funny rubbery texture. She liked the way it felt in her hands. She pointed, aimed, and shot.

"Nothing but net," said a Wishling boy admiringly. "Hey. I'm Tony. Who are you?"

"I'm Astra," she answered. "The new girl. I enjoyed playing your netball game."

Tony laughed. "It's called basketball, you know."

Wish Mission 8, Wishworld Observation #1: Wishlings have funny names for their games. There is no basket in basketball!

She then glanced at her Wish Pendant wristbands. Nothing. That was too bad. None of the netball—make that basketball—players was her Wisher. Astra had been distracted—again—by another one of the wonderful sports there. Now it was time to get down to business.

She looked around the yard. *Aha!* A girl was holding one of those fluffy white wishing flowers Lady Stella had told them about. Imagine if she was Astra's Wisher and she was just about to make her wish again! Astra ran over as the girl took a deep breath, ready to scatter the seeds.

"Hey!" Astra said eagerly. "Are you wishing for something?"

The girl lowered the arm holding the flower and gave Astra a dubious look. "Um, yeah," she said. "Why else would I be holding this dandelion?"

Wish Mission 8, Wishworld Observation #2: The fluffy white flowers Wishers wish on are called Dandy Lions.

"What's your wish?" Astra asked eagerly. "Is it a good one?"

The girl smiled. "I'll say. I wish I had a million dollars!" she said.

Astra frowned. A million! That was like a moonium! "All for yourself?" she asked.

The girl nodded.

"You wouldn't even share it?" Astra asked, trying to give the girl the benefit of the doubt.

"Nope," said the girl.

Astra gave her a disgusted look. "Well, that's not a good wish at all!"

The girl looked insulted. "Mind your own business!" she said. Then she raised her arm, closed her eyes, and blew. Astra watched as the fluffy seeds danced through the air across the schoolyard.

"Good luck with that one," muttered Astra to herself. She scanned the yard, counting the kids. Well, that girl obviously wasn't the person Astra was looking for. So who among the twenty-four remaining students was her Wisher?

A bell rang and the students all dropped what they were doing to line up and head inside. A black-and-white ball rolled up to Astra and she sent it flying with a well-placed kick. She smiled. She had been itching to do that! She joined the line and followed her class inside.

A young woman with her dark hair pulled into a ponytail was standing in the doorway, watching everyone head inside. Astra realized she must be her teacher. "I am Astra Starling. I am your new student," she told her.

"You are Astra Starling. You are my new student," the teacher repeated, just as Astra had known she would. "I am Ms. Lopez," she told her. "Head inside, Astra, it's time for lunch!" She sniffed the air. "And if I am not mistaken, it smells like they're making banana cream pie, lucky you!"

Astra smiled. There was something really nice about reminding adults of their favorite treats from childhood. It seemed always to bring a wistful smile to their faces.

The class trooped in through the cafeteria doors and Astra followed close behind. She had been warned that cafeterias on Wishworld were not up to Starling Academy standards, but she wasn't prepared for what she saw once she was inside: a dingy room with scuffed floors lined with bare tables. She grabbed a beat-up orange plastic tray and waited in line as a lady handed out plates of weird-looking food. Limited choices. No cloth napkins. And certainly no Bot-Bot waiters.

"I wish . . ." a boy ahead of Astra said.

In her eagerness, Astra nearly knocked down a curly-haired girl who stood between them. "You wish what?" she asked him.

The boy grinned. "If I tell you, it won't come true."

Astra shook her head. "Huh? Where did you get a crazy idea like that? That is not true!"

He arrived at the counter and peered through the foggy glass at the lunch offerings. "Hey, look, I got my wish!" he said.

Astra's heart leaped. "You did?"

"Yeah—pizza bagels!" he said excitedly.

"Pizza bagels?" Astra repeated. She had learned about both pizza and bagels in school, and she was certain they were two different things. But he pointed to a round food item covered in red sauce and some melted cheese. Astra frowned. What a waste of a wish! Still, she ordered one for herself. Might as well see what all the fuss was about. Once she had her food she looked around the crowded cafeteria for a seat.

"Hey, new girl, over here!" someone called. Astra smiled, headed to Tony's table, and sat down. "This is Timmy, Sean, Roseanne, Eleni, Janice, and Stephen," he said.

"Star—I mean, hello," said Astra. She glanced at her wristbands, which, unfortunately, were still dark.

"Astra's new," he explained.

Rebecca gave her a funny look. "Who starts school two weeks before summer vacation?" she asked, peeling the top off a container of something pink and creamy and licking it.

"Did you just move here?" asked Timmy.

Astra smiled. "I just arrived!" she said.

Too many questions! As Astra ate her pizza bagel (which was surprisingly tasty), she steered the subject to basketball, which was a good choice, as the kids all had a lot of opinions on the subject. She was relieved when the bell rang for class. She dumped her tray and headed to her new classroom. She was relieved to see that her wristbands began to glow as soon as she passed through the doorway, so she knew she was in the right place.

Once Astra was settled at a desk and had been given a math book, they started their lessons. The other Star Darlings hadn't mentioned just how tedious Wishling classes were. Math was especially painful, as Wishlings were terribly slow at figuring out the answers. She thought she might scream. They didn't know anything! In English class she thought she'd get to read some Wishworld lighterature, but instead they diagrammed sentences, which seemed startacularly silly. Did Wishlings really need to know this stuff?

Suddenly, class was interrupted as a voice, loud and crackly, came over the loudspeaker: "ATTENTION, STUDENTS. We have two announcements to make this afternoon. There will be a gymnastics competition this Friday after school in the gymnasium. Don't forget to come and cheer on your fellow students as they tackle the parallel bars, floor routines, the vault, and the uneven bars!"

Competition! Astra perked up. She had no idea what gymnastics was, but she was certain she was going to find out.

The announcements continued. "And on Saturday morning at eleven a.m., please join us for an art show in the lunchroom. Support your fellow student artists and check out some really beautiful and inspiring art they've been working on!"

Out of the corner of her eye she could see a serious-looking girl with curly brown hair jotting something down in her notebook. Astra's pulse quickened. The gymnastics competition was the key to her mission; she was sure of it!

"Time for science," said Ms. Lopez. "Have a great rest of the day, guys." The class packed up their backpacks, pushed in their chairs with a maximum of noise and effort, and headed out the door.

In the science room, Astra walked up to the teacher, a tall thin man in a long white coat. Oddly, he was missing hair from the top of his head.

"I am Astra, the new student," she told him.

"You are Astra, the new student," he said. He smiled at her and sniffed the air, looking wistful.

The students all sat down at tables in pairs. Astra stood at the front of the room uncertainly, not sure where she should go.

"Astra," said the teacher, "it looks like Emma's partner is absent today. Emma, will you wave so Astra can join you?"

Emma waved. To Astra's delight, she was the

curly-haired girl from across the aisle—the one who had been writing in her notebook during the announcements. *This could be it*, Astra thought. She took a deep breath. She was ready.

"Hey, Astra," Emma said, holding out her hand. Astra stared at it, not sure what to do. Then she slapped it, as she had seen the basketball players do earlier.

Emma blinked at her in surprise. "Oh, okay," she said with a shrug. "So it's nice to meet you." Then she said, "Wow." Both she and Astra stared as Astra's wristbands began to glow brightly.

"And it is extremely great to meet you," Astra said. "You have no idea."

CHAPTER
7

"So tell me all about your—" Astra began.

"Shhh!" said Emma. "Mr. Tedesco is about to start!"

"Greetings, students," said Mr. Tedesco. "Today we are going to learn how to build a catapult." He paused. "Can anyone tell me what a catapult is?"

Astra raised her hand. She knew that one and was eager to impress her Wisher with the knowledge she had gained in Wishers 101. "It's a magazine with pages full of things that you can purchase with paper money," she said confidently.

The class laughed. Astra scowled, but when she saw Emma grinning at her, she realized that the kids thought she was saying it to be funny. She laughed along, to show that she was a good sport.

Mr. Tedesco smiled. "Actually, that's a cata*log*. But that was a good guess, Astra." He looked around the room. "Has anyone heard of a catapult?"

Tony raised his hand. "It's a machine that launches things!" he said. "Like when you're attacking a castle. Flaming hot tar right over the walls!"

"That's exactly right, Tony," said Mr. Tedesco. He then projected an image of a strange machine on the whiteboard. "Catapults were widely used during medieval times. As you can see," he said, pointing to the different parts, "a catapult has a lever for pulling back and a fulcrum for rotation. When released, the catapult flings objects—or flaming liquids, in Tony's case—and they can go over walls and travel distances. We are going to build our own catapults in class today and then demonstrate them. We are going to learn all about force and its effect on speed and distance with this project. Plus it's a lot of fun to shoot things in class, isn't it?"

The class laughed.

"Very cool," said a girl with pale hair.

It was no wonder Astra had never heard of a catapult. Starland was a peaceful place and there was no need for weapons of any kind.

The teacher handed out shoe boxes, rulers, markers, tape measures, rubber bands, tape, plastic spoons, and a few small white objects to all the student pairs. Astra squeezed one of the small white things. It was soft. She smelled it. *Mmmmm.* Sweet, too. "Are these edible?" she asked Emma.

"Um, yeah," said the girl, giving her a funny look. "Marshmallows usually are."

While they began figuring out how to assemble their catapult, Astra tried to engage Emma in conversation. But she soon discovered that her partner was extremely single-minded when it came to schoolwork. While it was admirable, it was also pretty frustrating.

"Astra," Emma said. "Less talk, more . . . catapulting."

"As soon as you are done, you should try out your catapults," said Mr. Tedesco. "Shoot your marshmallow, measure the distance it travels, record the distance, and make any changes to your machines to see if you can shoot the marshmallows farther. Take careful notes on your work sheets. They are due tomorrow."

Suddenly, Astra had a great idea. If she worked super slowly and made lots of mistakes, she and Emma would have to work on the project that night after school. So she deliberately measured incorrectly, put the spoon on backward, and ate the marshmallows for good measure.

Emma looked frustrated. "Let's get this done," she said. "I have a lot going on after school today."

The bell rang. School was over for the day. And they still weren't close to finished. Astra was thrilled.

"I can't believe we have to finish that stupid catapult tonight," Emma moaned, shaking her head as they stood by her locker after school. "Like I don't have enough to do."

Astra leaned forward. "Sounds like you are very busy and wish for a more peaceful life of harmony and quietude," she said, stealing a few of Piper's phrases.

"Not really," said Emma. "That sounds kind of boring, actually."

Oh, well. Astra tried again. "So where are you going after school?" Astra asked. "Can I come?"

Emma shook her head. "Sorry," she said. "I've got gymnastics practice. Why don't I come to your house after I'm done? It's got to be quieter than my house!"

Astra had to think fast. "Um . . . my parents are working late tonight," she said.

"Isn't anyone going to be home? Do you have any brothers or sisters?" Emma asked.

"No, just me," said Astra. She had no idea why she had said that. But it sounded really appealing, actually. No little siblings getting in your stuff, stealing the attention from you and your accomplishments with their distracting cuteness. "Yeah," she went on. "It's just me and my parents. I have this whole huge room to myself. And my parents have all the time in the world for me. It's pretty great."

Emma smiled. "It sounds nice," she said. "I bet it's quiet, too. And that you never get compared to anyone. Nothing to live up to. You can just be yourself."

Astra nodded. "And since you're the only one, you never need to babysit or anything."

So Emma and Astra went their separate ways, promising to meet later at Emma's house. Astra teleported herself to town, popping into and out of shops. She could have spent all evening in the sporting goods store, trying out each piece of equipment while an extremely helpful salesperson explained how it all worked. Then she glanced at her Star-Zap and realized it was time to meet Emma. Her Star-Zap leading the way, she walked along the sidewalk, past homes with neat lawns and well-trimmed hedges, until she reached a cozy house with a swing on the porch and window boxes with pretty pink flowers cascading out of them. She walked up the steps and knocked on the door. Emma answered it.

"Hey, Astra," she said. "Come in." Astra stepped inside. The walls of the small entryway were jam-packed with photos of girls with medals and trophies, and it looked like the very same medals and trophies sat on the entryway table. Intrigued, Astra paused to take a look.

"Come on, we need to get started," said Emma, pulling her by the arm (a little forcefully, Astra thought) into the living room.

They walked into the kitchen, where Emma's mom was preparing dinner.

"Mom, this is Astra," said Emma. "She's new at school."

"Pleased to meet you," said Emma's mom, extending her hand. As before, Astra slapped it.

Emma's mom looked surprised for a moment, then laughed. "Oh, okay," she said. "So will you be joining us for dinner, Astra?"

"I'd love to," said Astra.

"We're having eggplant parmigiana," Emma's mom said. She paused for a moment. "Does anyone else smell cream puffs?" she asked. Emma and Astra both shook their heads.

Emma rooted around in the cupboard until she found a half-eaten bag of marshmallows. She shoved it under her arm and they headed upstairs to her bedroom to do their homework. The room was filled with colorful paintings, drawings, and sculptures. They knelt on the flowered rug, finished assembling their catapult, shot it, and measured the distance the marshmallow traveled. Then they learned that by tightening the rubber bands and adjusting the position of the spoon, they could make it go even farther. That time the marshmallow went so far it hit the opposite bedroom wall, knocking over a bottle that was sitting on a dresser. Astra walked over and picked up the bottle. She blinked. It was the polish of removal! Her eyes lit up. "Hey, can I have this?" she asked, holding up the bottle.

Emma shrugged. "Sure, I guess," she said.

"St—I mean thank you! Thank you!" Astra gushed, making sure the cap was on tightly before putting it carefully into her backpack. One bottle down, nine to go! They wrote down their observations.

"Cool," said Emma when they were done. "That wasn't so bad after all."

They had math homework, too, so they went straight to work on it. Astra watched as Emma stuck out her tongue in concentration as she worked. Astra knew all the answers, but she labored over them so Emma wouldn't get suspicious. She made sure that they finished at the same time.

Astra was ready to get to the bottom of the wish situation. "So tell me—" she started.

"Emma!" called her mom. "Have you finished your homework? Come help me with dinner! Your dad and sisters will be home soon!"

"Coming!" shouted Emma. She stood and turned to Astra. "Wanna help?"

Downstairs, Emma's mom pointed to a pile of vegetables and a white board. "Here, help me make the salad," she said.

Emma grinned. "My mom hates making salad," she told Astra.

"I do!" said her mom. "All that washing and chopping!"

"You can peel and slice those carrots," Emma said, pointing to the end of the counter, where two bowls sat. One was filled with yellow food and the other was filled with orange food. *Oh, starf!* she thought. *Which ones are the carrots?*

Wish Mission 8, Wishworld Observation #3: Add an "Identifying Wishworld Food" tutorial to avoid awkward situations like this!

Well, she had a fifty-fifty chance of getting it right. So Astra separated one of the yellow things from the rest. She pulled the stem on top and the peel began to separate from the inside pretty easily.

Emma glanced at what she was doing. "Astra, why

are you peeling a *banana*?" she asked. Then she started laughing. "You're so funny!"

"Ha-ha," Astra said. Yikes, she had to think fast! "Imagine mixing up a banana and a carrot. That is so silly!" She picked up the banana. "Mmmmm, what a tasty carrot," she said, taking a big bite. Emma and her mother exchanged amused glances. *Not bad*, thought Astra as she chewed. The banana had a soft interior and a mild, pleasant taste. Then she picked up a carrot and stared at it. She grabbed the green fronds at the top and gave them a tug, but it did not peel like the banana had. Now she was stumped. This was getting very uncomfortable.

Emma laughed and laughed. "That's so funny, pretending you don't know how to peel a carrot. Is that how you get out of helping in the kitchen at home?" She handed Astra a knife and a soft round reddish-orange food item. "Here, you can slice this tomato. I'll peel the carrots." She grabbed a utensil and began scraping the skin off them. *Whew! That was a close one!* Astra thought.

A bell dinged and Emma's mom put on some extremely large mittens, opened the oven door, and pulled out a bubbling dish. It looked pretty messy, all gooey and saucy, but it smelled startacularly good.

"Hello! I'm home!" someone called. A large man strode into the kitchen in a matching jacket and pants, a long strip of fabric tied around his neck. He was followed by a smallish girl in a zippered jacket with a hood and matching pants, her hair in a sleek bun.

"Hey, honey," Emma's mom said to the man, who was presumably her husband. "How was practice, Elizabeth?" she asked the little girl.

"It was great!" Elizabeth said. "I finally perfected my aerial!"

"Daddy!" cried Emma, lunging forward to hug him around his middle.

"Hello, sweetums, how was school today?" he asked, patting her head.

"Fine," she told him. "This is my new friend Astra."

Astra smiled. She liked that.

"Hello, new friend Astra," said Emma's dad. "Pleased to meet you."

Astra extended her hand. Oddly enough, Emma's dad didn't slap it. He engulfed it in his large one and shook it up and down. Astra made an observation: some Wishlings slap hands and other Wishlings shake them. Emma started to say something.

"Can it wait a minute?" he said. "I want to go upstairs and get changed out of this monkey suit." Without waiting for her answer, he left the kitchen, and Astra could hear the steps creak as he bounded upstairs.

Emma's mom took out plates and silverware, and the three girls set the dining room table, then headed back to the kitchen for napkins. The front door opened again with a burst of excited chattering.

Astra looked at Emma. "My big sisters," Emma explained. "Eva and Ellie. They're twins." Two girls who looked exactly alike, dressed just like Elizabeth, crowded into the kitchen, kissing their mother, tousling their sisters' hair, grabbing carrot sticks, dropping bags and jackets on the kitchen table, and talking, talking, talking. They talked almost as much as Gemma, for stars' sake! Astra caught a few phrases—straddle, press handstand, dive roll, pike. None of it made any sense to her. But she was entranced by their energy and enthusiasm. Elizabeth joined in and told her big sisters about her aerial. They cheered and hugged her.

When they finally paused to take a breath, Emma introduced Astra to them.

"We're the gymnastics champs of Greendale High," said Eva.

"And I'm the top gymnast at Greendale Elementary," offered Elizabeth.

Emma leaned over to whisper in Astra's ear. "They never stop talking," she said. "And it's only ever about one thing. My entire family is obsessed with gymnastics."

"What *is* gymnastics, anyway?" Astra asked her.

Emma grinned. "That's a good one. Oh, Astra, you make me laugh!"

Emma's dad came back downstairs, dressed in Wishling relaxing clothes, and there were more hugs and greetings. They sat down to dinner and Astra found that she was famished. Her plate of eggplant parmigiana and salad disappeared quite quickly, and she eagerly refilled her plate when offered seconds.

After the twins filled in the family on every move they had completed successfully at practice, Elizabeth told the story, in painstaking detail, of her aerial. Meanwhile, Astra polished off her second helping.

Emma's parents nodded happily. "All it takes is determination and practice," her father said. He turned to Emma. "Right, my girl?"

"Right, Dad," said Emma, her eyes on her plate.

"We're so excited to go to your competition on Friday, Emma," her mother said.

"Yeah," said Emma quietly.

"How about a little more enthusiasm, young lady!" her father said. "That floor routine isn't going to perfect itself, you know."

Astra listened to all this with great excitement. It made perfect sense to her now. Obviously, she had been chosen to go on this mission because of her love of sports. She wondered if Emma needed her help with the floor routine.

After dinner Elizabeth begged everyone to come outside to see her aerial. "And we can show you some of our moves," said Ellie.

Emma rolled her eyes. "How thrilling for you," she said.

But it *was* thrilling for Astra. It turned out that gymnastics was a variation of the advanced moves Astra did while playing a game of Poses—leaps and jumps and tumbles.

"Come join us!" said Eva.

Astra didn't need to be asked twice. Before she knew it, she was showing everyone her famous up-and-over starflip.

Someone started clapping. "You're good," said Emma's mom admiringly.

"Wow!" said Ellie. "You just did a perfect roundoff back-handspring back tuck. Emma!" she shouted. "You need to see this!"

But Emma was nowhere to be found.

"Oh, she's probably up in her room," said Elizabeth.

"She doesn't like gymnastics?" Astra asked, confused. "But I thought she was on the school team."

Eva lowered her voice. "Oh, she's just freaking out because she totally choked at the last meet."

Elizabeth did another perfect aerial and landed right in front of Astra. "Yeah, she blew it for her team. They lost because of her. She was really upset."

Ellie looked at her parents, who were talking to each other quietly. "My dad took it really hard."

"Well, he *was* the gymnastics champ in high school," said Eva. "He almost made it to nationals. But he lost out by one point. He doesn't want the same thing to happen to any of us."

Astra headed upstairs. She found Emma lying on her bed, staring up at the ceiling.

"Hi," said Astra.

"My dad is so proud of my sisters," Emma said sadly, "and I wish that . . ." Her voice trailed off.

"And you wish he was proud of you, too," Astra finished.

She felt a tingle of electricity down her spine. She had figured out the Wisher *and* the wish on the very same day! Things could not be going any better.

CHAPTER 8

Astra woke up, and for a brief moment she had no idea where she was. She looked around and saw that she was surrounded by paintings and drawings. *Oh, that's right.* She was in Emma's bedroom, wrapped up in something called a sleeping bag. Simply by saying "Hey, wouldn't it be a great idea if I slept over for the next three nights?" to Emma's mother, she had received an enthusiastic invitation. Emma's sisters had been confused ("You never let *my* friends stay over for three nights in a row!" Elizabeth had wailed. "And on a school night, too!"), and Emma had been delighted. Astra was certain she would be taking off right after Friday afternoon's meet and wouldn't need that third night, but she had added it just to be safe.

She yawned and stretched, feeling well rested and content. Her first day had gone extremely well. She'd made some interesting Wishworld observations, met her Wisher, and confirmed the wish. She knew that Emma's father would be incredibly proud of Emma when she helped her team to victory on Friday afternoon. Nobody knew more about competition, concentration, and training than Astra did. It was the perfect mission for her. They could just start creating that holo-statue in her likeness right now.

Emma was still asleep, so Astra considered her next steps. It seemed pretty simple: she'd just have to make sure that the girl went to all her practices, wasn't distracted, ate well, got plenty of sleep, worked hard, showed up at the meet, and did her best. Her father was sure to be impressed—and, most important, *proud* of his daughter.

School that day was pretty uneventful. Astra was just going through the motions, waiting for gymnastics practice that afternoon, where her real work would begin. At last the final bell rang. Astra and Emma grabbed their backpacks and headed to the locker room to change for practice.

"So I can't wait to see that floor routine of yours,"

Astra was saying as they walked down the hallway. Just then, a classroom door opened and an adult Wishling stepped out. She was a tall, thin woman with long, curly brown hair. Emma stopped right in her tracks.

"Well, hello there!" the woman said pleasantly. "I'm so happy to see you, Emma."

"Hi, Ms. Gonzales," Emma said—somewhat nervously, Astra noted. She looked both happy and a little apprehensive at the same time.

"Are you coming to art club this afternoon?" Ms. Gonzales asked. "There's still time to—"

"Sorry," Astra interrupted. She had this covered. Emma didn't need any distractions. "Emma has gymnastics practice today. There's a big meet coming up on Friday. Maybe she can come to your club after it's over."

Ms. Gonzales frowned. "But the . . ."

Astra grabbed Emma's arm and began to steer her down the hall. Who was that woman, and why was she trying to interfere with Emma's wish? "We're late for practice," Astra called over her shoulder. "See you later!"

There were other girls milling about in the locker room, already dressed in various uniforms, when they arrived. Astra wanted to use the Wishworld Outfit Selector, but she had no idea what to wear. Rather than make Emma suspicious, she pretended she needed to use the bathroom and wandered around the locker room trying to figure out what gymnasts wore.

"Is that a gymnastics uniform?" she asked a girl in a brimmed hat, striped pants, and a short-sleeved jersey. A large brown glove was tucked under her arm.

The girl gave Astra a funny look. "Softball," she said. "That's a joke, right?"

Astra moved on. "Do you play gymnastics?" she asked a girl in a tight-fitting outfit that covered only her torso, her hair tucked under a tight rubber hat. The girl gawked at her.

"No, I play swimming," the girl finally answered. "Are you for real?"

Another girl took pity on Astra. "I'm on the gymnastics team," she said. "Can I help you?"

Astra took in her one-piece outfit with long sleeves and bare legs. "You already have," she told her.

Astra ducked into a bathroom stall and flipped through the outfits on her Wishworld Outfit Selector until she found what she was looking for. She picked a red one with a pretty multicolored star on the front. She stepped up to the mirror and took a look. Perfect.

She found Emma, who was similarly dressed, shoving

her school clothes and books into a locker. "Cute leo-tard," Emma told her.

"It *is* a cute leotard," Astra said.

They walked into the gym and Astra was instantly in heaven. The room was filled with all sorts of equipment. There were girls flipping and spinning and vaulting and jumping. Astra introduced herself to the coach ("I am Astra. I am the new girl on your team.") and found out that her favorite childhood dessert was something called brownies. Before the coach could blink, Astra was on the mat, showing off her up-and-over starflip. Make that her roundoff back-handspring back tuck. This was amazing. Not only was she making a wish come true; she was learn-ing a new sport, which just happened to be one she had a natural talent for. She kept an eye on Emma, who was working on her floor routine. Astra learned how to do an aerial. It was going to come in very handy during her next game of Poses; that was for sure.

She especially enjoyed when she was able to take a break and shout encouragement at Emma, who looked like she could use some. When practice ended for the day, they pulled sweatpants on over their leotards (Emma loaned her a pair), laced up their sneakers, grabbed their backpacks, and headed out the exit door.

"Surprise!" said someone from the curb. The girls spun around.

Emma's face lit up. "Daddy!" she cried. "What are you doing here?"

"I thought I would take you girls out to dinner," he said.

"Can we go to Chewsy Cheese?" Emma asked excitedly.

"Of course," he said. "Grilled cheese and a root beer float, am I right?"

"You know it," Emma said. She slipped her hand into his. "Come on, Astra, my dad is taking us out to dinner!"

They drove to a nearby restaurant, which was lit up with multicolored blinking lights. Inside it was crowded and loud. Astra loved it immediately.

Astra stared at the menu. There were cheeseburgers, cheese sticks, cheese omelets, cheese fries, cheesecake, and twenty different kinds of grilled cheese.

The waitress came over. "May I take your order?" she asked. Astra stared at her hat, which looked like a large block of cheese.

"Is that made of real cheese?" Astra asked, her eyes wide. This warranted an observation.

Everyone laughed. "Oh, Astra," said Emma's dad,

shaking his head. "You're too funny." He ordered a cheeseburger, fries, and coffee.

"I'll have a grilled cheese with tomato on rye and a root beer float," said Emma.

Hmmm. Sounded good. "Me too," said Astra.

The waitress returned with a steaming mug of coffee. Emma's father ripped open a paper package and poured some grainy stuff into it, stirring it with a spoon. Meanwhile, Emma pulled some colored pencils out of her schoolbag, flipped over her menu, and began drawing on it.

Her dad took a sip of his coffee, pronounced it quite tasty, and began peppering his daughter with questions.

Had she tried her best that day? Yes, she had.

Was she perfecting her floor routine? She was working on it.

What did the coach have to say? Nothing much.

Did she think she was ready for Friday's meet? Sure.

Emma's dad sighed and ran his hand through his hair. Emma's answers were apparently not satisfactory. Astra noticed that she seemed pretty distracted. Emma's dad turned to Astra, clearly frustrated.

"What do you think, Astra? Is she working hard?" he asked.

"She is," said Astra. "I think she is going to do great on Friday, actually. You're coming, right?" she asked worriedly.

"Of course," said Emma's dad. "The whole family is going to be there. I just want to make sure that Emma is ready."

Emma continued sketching, as if she hadn't heard herself being discussed.

There was an uncomfortable silence. Luckily, the food came very quickly. "Here you go," said the waitress, setting the tray down on the edge of the table. "Grilled cheese with tomato on rye," she said, setting it before Astra.

Astra picked up one of the melty sandwich halves and took a tentative bite. Then another. It was positively delicious. She next took a sip of the root beer float, and it was sweet creamy goodness. *Almost as delicious as an egg cream*, she thought.

They ate their food in silence. When the plates were cleared, Emma went back to drawing.

"I had an idea, sweetheart," Emma's dad said.

Emma looked up expectantly. "Yes?" she said.

"Astra is really good at roundoff back-handspring back tucks. Maybe she could teach it to you. You could add it to your floor routine," he suggested. "That might really put you over the edge."

"Maybe," said Emma quietly. She went back to her paper.

Emma's dad sighed again. "Can you stop doodling for a minute and talk to me?" he asked. "I don't think that you are taking this meet as seriously as you should. Your sisters seem to understand how important it is. Heck, Elizabeth is already doing—"

"Dad, I need to ask you . . ." Emma interrupted.

Just then, the waitress came over with the check. Emma's dad stood up.

"In a minute, sweetheart. I'm going to go pay the bill."

Emma scowled and crumpled the menu. Astra put a hand on her friend's arm. Emma shook her off.

"He just doesn't get it," she complained. "I want to win the meet, of course, but there's something else that's more important. . . ."

"Yes, I understand," said Astra. "You want to make him proud of you."

"Yes, but . . ."

"But nothing," said Astra. "You have to believe in yourself, Emma. You have to focus on what is most important to you and not be distracted by the things that are not. Everything is going to work out great if you can just do that."

Emma sighed. "Fine," she said. She slid out of the booth and walked over to her dad. They spoke for a moment and he gave her a quick hug.

Astra gathered her backpack and, before she got up, leaned over and smoothed out the menu. She gasped. Emma had drawn Astra. She had gotten her hair, her upturned nose, the shape of her face, and the mischievous gleam in her eyes just right. It was a perfect likeness.

CHAPTER
9

Astra woke up, her eyes gleaming. It was Friday! How was she going to survive a full day of classes before the big meet? She was so excited about making Emma's wish come true and collecting the wish energy, and she was thrilled that she was going to be the first Star Darling who didn't need help on her mission. She wondered if that meant she would collect double the wish energy or something.

Emma's parents each gave her a big hug as she headed out the door. "Good luck!" they called. "We'll see you in the gym!"

Emma turned to wave from the sidewalk. "See you in the gym!" she called. She waited until they got to the end of the block, then turned to Astra. "Tell me again it's all going to be okay," she said.

Oh, no! Why was Emma so nervous? That wasn't helpful at all!

"It's all going to be okay," Astra said soothingly. But when Emma was looking the other way, she tapped her elbows together three times for good luck. With an attitude like that, she was pretty sure they needed it.

"Astra, are you paying attention?" Ms. Lopez asked during English class. "Can you please tell me which word in this sentence is the adjective?"

Astra blinked at her slowly, then stared at the board. "Um, roundoff?" she said. She had been running Emma's routine through her head step-by-step instead of paying attention.

The class laughed. Everyone, that is, but Emma. The very word seemed to make her ill.

"Do you mean rounded?" Ms. Lopez asked. She looked at Astra sympathetically. "I know you are excited about the gymnastics competition," she said, "but please try to pay attention for the rest of the day. It's not that much longer, I promise."

Astra nodded. She was a little disappointed that she wasn't going to be competing. How exciting would that have been! But there simply hadn't been enough time to teach her all of the events. So instead she had memorized Emma's floor exercise. She would show everyone when she got back home, which hopefully would be very soon.

Astra waved excitedly when Emma's family entered the gym. She wanted to sit with them so she could make sure that Emma's dad didn't miss a thing. She was counting on wrapping up the wish that day.

Astra sat between Emma's dad and Eva. She looked around the gymnasium. There were a couple of kids from her and Emma's class there. She gave them a wave. She was pleased to note that Ms. Lopez was there, too. The teacher looked at Astra and raised her thumb. Astra gasped. Back on Starland that was an extremely rude gesture, one that would certainly get you a detention, if not a suspension, especially if you did it to a teacher. But Ms. Lopez was looking back at her expectantly. So Astra gulped and returned the gesture. She burst into laughter. Wait till she told the rest of the Star Darlings that she had given a teacher a thumbs-up!

Eva explained how the meet worked. The teams each competed in four events—uneven bars, floor exercise, vault, and balance beam. The team with the highest overall score would be the winner. "I'm worried about Emma's floor exercise," Eva said. "She didn't get enough height in her tumbling pass last time."

Emma did well on the vault, balance beam, and uneven bars. Astra watched her with admiration as she soared through the air, effortlessly catching the bar in both hands, extending, releasing, and pirouetting. How she wished they had that kind of equipment on Starland! It was like flying!

Astra stole a glance at the scoreboard. Emma's team was doing well—but so was another team. Their scores were uncomfortably close. The floor exercises would settle that. There were two girls left to go from the top two teams . . . and Emma was one of them.

Eva buried her head in her hands. "Poor Emma," she said. "The pressure is going to get to her!"

The other team went first. The music began to play and the girl began with a tumbling pass that included a series of cartwheels. Her routine was nearly flawless.

Astra had been keeping a running score in her head. If Emma didn't get at least a nine point six two five, her team would lose. Eva turned to Astra. "I know this is confusing at first," she said, "but if Emma doesn't get at least a nine point six two five, her team will lose. Just like last time."

"Thanks," said Astra, hiding her smile. "It's so confusing!"

Eva clutched Astra's arm as Emma went through her routine. Leaping, tumbling, turning, twisting—she did it all perfectly. "This is it," said Eva. "She just needs to do her final tumbling pass and stick her landing."

Astra watched as Emma took a deep breath and began. But instead of doing a series of cartwheels as usual, she did a dive cartwheel into a roundoff back-handspring ending with a double back tuck! It was Astra's move! She felt so proud. But with such momentum, would Emma be able to stay within bounds and stick her landing? The crowd gasped as Emma bobbled for a moment, then quickly regained her balance, feet firmly planted beneath her, toes barely inside the line. The crowd erupted. As Emma's family stood and cheered, Astra stared at the scoreboard, holding her breath.

Then the score: 9.9!

"She did it!" Eva shouted. "She did it!"

Emma's parents hugged each other. Her sisters clapped and cheered some more. Emma's coach and her teammates jumped up and down. Emma had a small smile on her face. *Why isn't she happier?* Astra wondered. *Her wish is coming true.*

Emma's dad ran onto the gym floor, and Astra jumped up to follow and collect her energy. He picked Emma up and spun her around. "I am so proud of you," he said.

Proud. The magic word. Astra turned to Emma, ready for the onslaught of wish energy. She held out her wrists, a smile of eager anticipation on her face. But there was nothing. What was going on?

She looked up at Emma, who wore a wistful smile. She didn't look happy at all. She actually looked kind of sad.

Astra shook her head. "What's wrong?" she asked. "Your wish came true!"

Emma frowned. "*My* wish?" She laughed. "Maybe my father's wish, but not mine."

"But you said you wanted to make your father proud of you," Astra argued.

"Not this way," said Emma. She opened her mouth to speak, then shut it firmly. She shook her head. "Listen, I've got to go."

Dumbfounded, Astra watched Emma walk across the gym floor and out the door.

Astra glanced down at her Countdown Clock. It was still ticking. She didn't know what to do. She knew that she was wasting precious time. *How did I mess this up so badly?* she wondered. She thought and she thought and she could not come up with an answer.

She waved good-bye to Emma's family and sat there as the teams packed up and everyone left. She sat as the custodian moved all the equipment back to the corner of the gym and started sweeping the floor. And when he turned out the lights, she sat in the faint gloomy glow that came through the high gymnasium windows. She had no idea what to do.

Suddenly, there was a big bang as the heavy gym door swung open. Astra whipped her head toward the sound.

"Need a little help?" said a very familiar voice.

Astra could have wept with joy when she realized just who was making her way toward her in the darkened gymnasium.

"I do," she said, standing up in the bleachers. "I really do."

It was Libby. "Lady Stella sent me," she said gently. "Your energy levels were dropping and she started to get worried. You're running out of time."

"Thanks for pointing that out," said Astra sarcastically.

"Don't get mad at me," said Libby. "I'm here to help you."

Astra sighed. "I know. Star apologies."

"Why don't you just fill me in on everything that's happened so far?" Libby suggested, sitting down on the bleachers. So Astra did.

When she was finished talking, Libby sat in silence, digesting the information. Finally, she spoke. "So you confirmed that her wish was to make her father proud of her?"

Astra sighed. "Yes, she was very clear about it," she said.

"Exactly how much time is left?"

"Eighteen hours," said Astra.

"So that takes us to . . ."

"A little after one o'clock tomorrow," said Astra.

Then she heard a delicate snore. "Stay right there!" she said to Libby, who clearly wasn't going anywhere. Astra ran to the girls' bathroom and grabbed a couple of paper towels. She returned to the gym and rooted around in her backpack until she found the polish of removal. She poured some on a paper towel and began to scrub Libby's nails. It was very slow going, but finally, when the last nail was polish-free, Libby sat up.

"Where were we?" she asked. Astra held up the

now-empty bottle. Libby gave her a huge smile and looked down at her nails. "Star salutations, Astra," she said happily. "I feel so awake!"

"That's great," said Astra. "But what isn't so great is that we only have eighteen hours left—until one o'clock tomorrow."

"That seems like an odd deadline," said Libby. "Does something important happen at one o'clock tomorrow?"

Astra shook her head. "I just don't know."

"Hmmm . . . should we try to find Emma and ask her?" Libby asked.

Astra sighed. "Sure," she said dejectedly.

They walked into the hallway. Astra tore down a poster advertising the gymnastics meet. She reached for the next poster and stopped. "Moons and stars!" she said. She pointed to it.

"Oooh, paper," said Libby. "Pretty cool."

Astra shook her head. "No. Look." She pointed to the words:

ART SHOW!

20,000 LEAGUES UNDER THE SEA

SCHOOL CAFETERIA

SATURDAY AT 11:00 AM

But it was the last line that was the most important:

WINNERS ANNOUNCED AT 1:00 PM

It all came to her in a rush. "Emma's a great artist," she explained to Libby. "Her room is full of beautiful paintings and drawings, and someone—I guess it was the art teacher—was trying to get her to work on a project." Astra's face got warm as she remembered how dismissive she had been to the teacher. She shook her head, recalling Emma's words: *Not this way.* "Emma wanted her father to be proud of her, all right. But it wasn't for gymnastics. It was for her artwork. Moons and stars! How did I miss that?"

"So all we have to do is find her and convince her to submit something for the art show?" Libby asked. "When's Saturday, by the way?"

"I think it's tomorrow!" Astra answered. "And that's got to be it!" she added. "I think I know where she is. Follow me."

Astra led Libby down a hallway, then up a flight of stairs. She paused in front of a classroom door, waiting for Libby to catch up. She put her hand on the doorknob and quietly opened the door. There was Emma, standing in front of a large sculpture. She was concentrating so hard she didn't hear the girls enter the room. She had an expression on her face that Astra did not recognize. She almost gasped when she realized what it was—pure happiness.

"Oh, Emma," she said. "It's beautiful."

CHAPTER
18

And it was. Emma had created a large sculpture of a beautiful woman with wild, flowing hair. Astra took another look and blinked. Well, it was a beautiful woman from the waist up. From the waist down was a completely different story. It was some sort of odd creature.

"Wow," said Astra. "I really like your . . . sculpture."

"It's a mermaid," explained Emma. "I've been working on it for months, whenever I could find the time. I was hoping to have it done for the art show tomorrow." She shook her head. "But I never had time to finish."

Libby stepped up. "It's gorgeous," she said.

"This is my friend Libby," Astra explained. "From my old school."

"You're really talented," Libby said, studying the sculpture.

"Thank you," said Emma.

"What is it made out of?" Astra asked.

Emma's eyes were shining. "It's this special sand clay I made. The theme of the art show is 20,000 Leagues Under the Sea, and I remembered all the fun summers we had when I was little, building castles and digging in the sand. So I decided to do a sand sculpture." She paused and her shoulders sagged. "I didn't get it finished in time."

"Can't you finish your sculpture tonight and submit it tomorrow for the show?" Astra asked.

Emma shook her head. "No, I needed to go to the beach and gather rocks and shells and seaweed and stuff and decorate it. But with all the practices and meets, I could never get my parents to take me. I'm totally out of time. It's too late to finish it."

Astra's heart sank. If only she had truly listened to her Wisher, she might have been able to help her.

Suddenly, she had an idea. "Hey, Emma," she said. "What if I told you we could get you exactly what you need?"

Emma smirked. "I'd say you were crazy," she answered.

"Go home and have dinner with your family," said Astra. "Tell them about the art show and that they need to come. We'll take care of getting the stuff you need. You can finish it in the morning and enter it in the competition."

Emma looked like she was trying hard not to get excited. "You're sure? You're really sure? It sounds impossible."

"I'm sure," said Astra. "But don't wait up," she added. "This could take a while!"

"I think you're crazy, too," said Libby.

"That's because you don't know my special talent," said Astra. "It's teleporting!"

"Ooh," said Libby. "Now that's a good one to have."

The question was, would she be able to take Libby along with her? The two girls held hands as Astra wished. It did not work. They stood back to back and Astra tried again. No such luck. Astra was about to head off on her own when she had a sudden idea, inspired by her roommate. She engulfed Libby in a big hug. *I wish I was at the beach*, she thought. There was a *whoosh*, everything grew blurry, and there was a feeling of moving fast.

And suddenly, they were standing in the sand! They were surrounded by palm trees and crystal-blue waters. White foam flew as the surf crashed onto the shore. They took off their shoes and dug their toes into the soft, silky sand. Astra couldn't help herself: she did a cartwheel of joy. Then another.

"That's a new one," said Libby. "You're going to slay us all in Poses when you get back."

"As usual," said Astra cheekily. She looked around, taking it all in. "It really is amazing here," she said.

The girls raced to the water's edge, filling their pockets with all the treasures from the sea they could find—tiny whelk shells; bits of green and blue sea glass, their edges softened by the tides and the sand; driftwood weathered into interesting shapes and bleached by the sun. Libby gathered the edges of her skirt with one hand and filled the hollow with crab claws, sand dollars, and scallop shells.

Astra spotted something star-shaped in the surf and thought for a moment that her eyes were deceiving her. She reached down and cradled the creature in her palm. "Have you ever seen anything lovelier?" she asked.

"How startastic!" said Libby.

"Piper would love it," Astra said. The creature moved its legs gently in her hand. "I wish I could take it home." But she knew it needed to be returned to the sea. She waded out and gently placed the creature back in the water.

Then Astra got a sudden inspiration. She bent down and filled her arms with seaweed in all shapes and sizes— thin ribbons, wide sheets, curly bright green tendrils. They lay their treasures on the sand and began to fill Astra's backback. The sun was sinking, its golden pink rays settling over the horizon. "It's time to go back," Astra said.

"Hey," said Libby with a laugh. "One of my shells is making a run for it!" She pointed to a tiny spiral shell that was slowly sneaking away.

"That was a close one!" said Astra. "Let's make sure we're not taking anyone else for a ride!" They carefully checked their shells, then finished packing. They hugged each other and Astra wished that she was back at Emma's house. Luckily no one noticed two girls magically appearing in the middle of Emma's backyard.

As she walked up the stairs to Emma's room, Astra thought she would burst with excitement. She also felt hopeful. But worried, too. Time was running out. This was their only chance. Emma had to convince her father to go to the show, finish her sculpture, win the prize, and make her father proud.

This had to work; it just had to!

CHAPTER
11

When Astra woke up the next morning in her usual spot on the floor in the sleeping bag, she immediately sprang up to wake Emma.

But Emma was already gone.

On her pillow was a note.

Dear Astra & Libby,

I found the bag of sea stuff! I don't know how you did it, but thank you so so so much! I'm going straight to school to finish the sculpture, so meet me there.

Love, Emma

P.S.: I told my family about the art show last night. Fingers crossed that they make it!

"Good morning, Astra," said Emma's mom when Astra and Libby entered the dining room. "And nice to meet you, Libby. Emma told me you would be staying over. Is she sleeping in this morning?"

"She already left for the art show!" said Astra. She looked at the family, all eating bowls of cereal around the table. "So you all are going to come, right?"

Eva yawned. "Ellie and I have practice this morning," she said. "And, Mom and Dad, you promised you were going to come watch us."

"I did," Emma's dad said, nodding. "I guess I'll have to go see Emma's art another time."

Astra gulped. This wasn't exactly going the way she had imagined.

Emma's dad stood and headed into the kitchen to refill his coffee cup. Astra followed him. She knew how to make him come to the show. It wasn't ideal, but she couldn't be choosy at that point.

She cleared her throat and Emma's dad glanced at her. Looking deep into his eyes, she said: "You are going to Emma's art show this morning."

He frowned. "I don't think I'm going to be able to make it," he said. "You heard the girls. I promised to go to their gymnastics practice."

Astra stood there, blinking. The rules of hypnotizing adults were very confusing.

She followed him back into the dining room. Libby looked at her hopefully, and Astra shook her head. Libby grimaced.

Astra could feel herself getting angrier and angrier. This wasn't fair to Emma at all. Her family had all the time in the world for gymnastics, but they couldn't be bothered to go to her art show? That was wrong, wrong, wrong.

Before she realized what she was doing, she slammed her hand down on the dining room table.

"Listen up," she said.

Everyone stared at her, openmouthed. Elizabeth had been about to put some cereal into her mouth, and the spoon hovered in midair.

"This is really important to Emma. The most important thing in her life, believe it or not. She has given up so much to do what you guys like—gymnastics—and she did an amazing job yesterday. But art is her passion. And it would really mean so much to have you all there. You *have* to be there."

The family looked at each other. "I guess we could leave practice early," said Eva reluctantly.

"If it's that important to Emma, we'll be there," said her father.

"But Saturday mornings are my only days to watch cartoons!" whined Elizabeth.

"Too bad, short stuff," said Ellie. "Emma is always there for us. Now it's our turn to be there for her."

Emma's mom put her hand on top of Astra's. "Thank you, Astra," she said simply. "Now you can sit down and eat."

Whew. Astra felt relieved. After breakfast she and Libby ran upstairs to get dressed, then headed to the school. Now all that was left was to make sure Emma's sculpture was finished in time.

When they arrived, Ms. Gonzales, the art teacher, was there, as well. "Hello!" she said when she saw Astra and Libby. "I am so thrilled that Emma is going to enter the contest! I gather you two had something to do with it."

Astra smiled and nodded.

"Her sculpture is wonderful," the teacher continued. "So evocative of the sea and childhood diversions."

"Um, yeah," said Astra. "Exactly."

Emma turned to the two girls proudly. The mermaid

was nearly finished. She wore a necklace of crab claws. Two large scallop shells served as her bikini top. Her tail was covered with a stunning mosaic of shells, pieces of seaweed, and sea glass. It was startacularly beautiful.

Ms. Gonzales glanced at her watch. "I've got to go and welcome the judges," she said. "The show begins in ten minutes and all entries must be registered beforehand. So please don't be late."

"I'll be done in a minute," said Emma distractedly. She squinted at the sculpture. "Something is missing. . . ." She grabbed some of the ribbony seaweed and artfully entwined it in the mermaid's flowing hair.

Astra grinned. "That's it. Perfect!"

It took the three of them to lift the sculpture and carry it down the hallway toward the auditorium.

"Be careful! Don't drop her!" Astra said warningly. When they successfully reached the auditorium, she peered through the doors, where she could see Ms. Gonzales, chatting with the judges and looking around nervously for Emma.

"Here we come," said Astra. She leaned her back against the door and pushed it—but it wouldn't budge.

"Hurry, Astra, this is getting heavy!" said Libby.

Astra pushed again. Then, after making sure the two girls could hold the sculpture on their own, she let go of it and pulled. She tried the other door. "I can't open it!" she cried.

"This is the only way in," Emma said. "It's got to open!"

Emma looked at the clock on the wall. "We're running out of time!" she cried.

Libby took a step backward. There was a strange sickly gray mist surrounding the door handle. *What in the world*—

She touched the mist and shivered. "It's so cold!" she said, rubbing her hands on her skirt for warmth.

"What's going on?" asked Emma. "I can't see!"

Something very strange was going on. It was almost as if something—or someone—was deliberately trying to keep them out.

Emma was near tears. "We're going to miss registration!" she said. "We have to get in there!"

Just then, Libby got a funny look on her face. "I'm not quite sure why I am doing this," she said, "but reach into my pocket. . . ."

Astra did and her fingers closed around an angular pink stone—Libby's Power Crystal!

"Put it on the door," instructed Libby.

"Put what on the door?" asked Emma, her view blocked by the large sculpture. "What is going on?"

To Astra's and Libby's amazement, the gray mist shrank back and disappeared.

"What's happening?" Emma demanded. "What are you doing?"

Before they could figure out how to answer her, the door opened with a snap.

The Star Darlings looked at each other. They had no idea what had just happened, but they realized it was something very big indeed.

Would Emma's wish come true? Or was Astra destined to be a wish energy failure?

CHAPTER
12

Astra, Emma, and Libby raced to the registration table (well, as quickly as three girls carrying a very heavy sculpture could race), arriving just in time.

"A minute longer and you wouldn't have made it," said the judge.

Afterward, Emma placed her sculpture on a folding table. A crowd began to gather around it. But Emma didn't notice.

She scanned the room excitedly. "Where is my dad?" she asked. Astra looked around but couldn't find him. Emma's shoulders sagged. "He forgot," she said. "He only cares about gymnastics."

Emma moped in the corner while Astra and Libby

examined the rest of the entries. The judges roamed the room, taking notes and consulting each other. Astra tried to eavesdrop and briefly wished that her special talent was super hearing.

There were many visitors to the art show. But Emma's family was nowhere to be found.

Astra sighed.

"We tried. We couldn't have tried harder," Libby assured her.

A crowd began to gather around the judges' table. One of the judges stepped up to the microphone. She gave a speech about art and creativity and effort, which Astra didn't really listen to. She was too upset. Emma reached out and squeezed her hand. "Thanks for everything," she said.

"And the winner is . . ." The judge paused, holding up a shiny gold medal on a bright red ribbon.

"Emma Prendergast!"

Despite the fact that her Wish Mission was foiled, Astra squealed and jumped up and down with joy. Emma threw her arms around Astra and Libby.

"You won!" shouted Astra. "You did it!"

"*We* did it," said Emma, her eyes shining. "I couldn't have done it without you."

"Go up and get your medal!" Libby shouted.

Emma looked around the room and her face fell. "What's the point?" she said bitterly. "My family didn't come. All they care about is gymnastics. They just don't care about anything else."

"Emma! Emma!" someone called. Emma and Astra spun around. Emma's father was trying to fight his way through the crowd to his daughter. "That's my girl!" he shouted.

Emma's face broke into a huge grin. Her dad made his way to her side and scooped her up in a big hug. Suddenly, the rest of her family was there, too, hugging and kissing her.

"I had no idea how important this was to you," he said. "All I could ever think about was gymnastics."

"It's okay, Daddy," Emma said.

"No, it isn't," he said. "It wasn't fair to you at all." He took a deep breath. "Your mother and I were talking on the way here. Now that we know what is really important to you, if you want to quit gymnastics, that's fine with us."

"I'll never quit gymnastics," said Emma. "I like it. Just not as much as the rest of you. But maybe I'll cut back a bit so I can go to art club, too."

He tousled her hair. "I'm really proud of you, sweetheart. Really proud."

Astra and Libby both watched, openmouthed, as the rainbow arc of pure wish energy danced around the room joyously before being absorbed into Astra's wristbands.

Libby smiled gently at Astra. "Great job," she said. "But you know what happens now. We have to go."

Astra sighed. "I know," she said sadly. She had heard from other Star Darlings that it can be very difficult to leave once you get to know your Wisher so well. But it felt even worse than she expected it to.

Emma bounded over. "I got my wish!" she said. "My dad is so proud of me. For my art! I've never been so happy in my life. Thank you so much!"

"I'm so glad for you," said Astra. "I'm just sorry that it took me so long to figure out what you wanted. I was telling you to be a gymnast when you really wanted to be an artist. I'm sorry I wasn't more helpful."

"Don't be crazy," said Emma. "You told me to believe in myself. And to focus on what was most important to me and not be distracted by the things that were not important. I couldn't have done this without you. You helped me more than you'll ever know. How can I repay you?"

"Oh, don't be silly," said Astra.

Libby poked her in the back and pointed to her fingernails.

"Well, now that you mention it," said Astra, "could you give me some polish of removal? About nine bottles should do it."

Epilogue

Astra stood in the starmarble hallway, waiting to be summoned into Lady Stella's office. She knew she was mere starmins away from getting her very own Power Crystal, which—she had seen firsthand—had some pretty startastic powers. But why did she feel so nervous?

Only one thing would make her feel better. She flipped open her Star-Zap and placed a holo-call. Instantly, a holo-picture appeared in front of her.

"Astra!" her mother cried happily. "We were just talking about you. It's just not the same without you here."

"Hi, Mom," Astra said, her voice nearly breaking. "Hey, everyone."

Her family was sitting in the gathering room. Her brother and sister were playing a game of Aughts and

Naughts. They all paused what they were doing to wave to her.

"We really do miss you," said Asia. "And I was just kidding. I'm going to keep our room just the way you left it."

"So how is school?" asked her father. "Anything new and exciting?"

Astra smiled. "School is good. I'll tell you all about it. Someday."

Lady Stella's door slid open and the headmistress stood there, smiling kindly at Astra. "We're ready for you," she said.

"Who's that?" asked her brother. "Are you in trouble?"

"I'm not in trouble, don't worry," said Astra. "I've just got to go."

"Bye!" they shouted.

"Bye, everyone," she said. She suddenly felt glad that she wasn't an only child (today, at least), and even though her family didn't quite get her drive and ambition, she felt loved and appreciated. That was what really mattered anyway. She snapped her Star-Zap shut and followed Lady Stella through the door.

Astra walked to the Lightning Lounge with Piper, admiring her newly acquired Power Crystal, a quarrelite. It glowed with a red-hot intensity, and sparks of energy raced across the asteroid-shaped stone. She was starprised at how much she was enthralled by her jewel. Accessories were always just distractions before, things to get in the way, or possibly get lost, while she played her beloved sports. But this was different. The Power Crystal was breathtakingly beautiful, of course, but it was mostly, she thought, because she had earned it herself and because there was deep meaning behind it—an obstacle faced and overcome, a job well done.

Piper understood. "It's starmazing, isn't it?" she said simply. Astra nodded.

They stepped up to the door of a private room and slid it open. As soon as Astra stepped into the room the Star Darlings swarmed her. Everyone was desperate to take off the polish. Astra started handing out bottles.

"It smells terrible!" said Cassie as she unscrewed the top from the bottle of nail polish remover.

"It's so weirdly cold!" said Adora.

After a few minutes of rubbing and scrubbing . . .

"I feel so much better," said Adora.

"Me too," said Clover.

"You can hear me!" Adora cried.

"I'll never skip again," said Scarlet with a shudder. "How humiliating."

"Hey, where's Leona?" Tessa asked. She reached into the bowl of star snacks and pulled out a mooncheese crisp. She popped it into her mouth. "Mmmm, delicious," she said. "If I never eat another Moonberry, I'll be startastically content!"

"I have no idea," said Cassie. "Was she at the ceremony?"

Vega rewound her holo-vid and shook her head.

"Say something, Vega," Piper begged.

"What do you want me to say? I have no words upon this day," Vega said.

Piper's face fell.

"Just kidding!" Vega said. "Oh my stars, you should have seen your face! Was it really as bad as all that?"

"Worse," said Piper.

The door slid open forcefully and Leona ran inside, her golden curls wilder than ever. She had a broad smile on her face.

"I have terrible news!" she said. "We tracked down Ophelia while you were gone!"

"And this is terrible . . . how?" asked Cassie.

Astra glanced down at Leona's golden fingernails. *Of course!* She grabbed the girl's hands and scrubbed until her nails were bare.

Leona nodded and smiled. "Great news, huh?"

"How did you find her?" Cassie wanted to know. "And is she an orphan?"

Piper spoke up. "I remembered you had said that Lady Stella thought that the orphanage had a different name. So we went to Vega . . ."

Vega took up the story. "And I had holo-vidded the conversation, of course, so I rewound it and we got the name."

"Turns out it's a real school in Starland City," Leona broke in. "So we went there. We couldn't find Ophelia, but we left her a message. And she just sent me a holo-text saying that she's going to call any starmin now!"

Leona's Star-Zap began to flicker and chime. "It's her!" she cried, accepting the call. Ophelia's tiny self, with her ocher eyes huge and serious, appeared in the air.

"Hi, everyone!" she said.

Everyone waved to her as they clustered around Leona.

"I just wanted to say I am sorry," said Ophelia. "For misleading you and for pretending to be someone I wasn't."

"I knew it!" said Cassie and Scarlet at the same time.

"But why did you lie, Ophelia?" said Leona. "I thought we were friends."

"I had to," said Ophelia. "I had my stars set on going to Starling Academy. But my grades weren't so stellar."

"I'll say," said Scarlet.

"And I bombed the entrance exam. I somehow managed to get an interview, but that didn't go so well, either. I was devastated."

Ophelia continued. "Then I got a holo-communication from Starling Academy. There was a spot open. But I was told that it was intended for a special student, an orphan. But they couldn't find one. So I just needed to pretend I was an orphan if I wanted to go there. I thought it was strange, but I just did as I was told."

She took a deep breath. "Once I arrived at Starling Academy I got a message every morning that told me what to do. Act like a sad orphan. Report back on everything you all said and did. Make friends with Leona." She had the good grace to look ashamed. "Sorry, Leona," she said. "I really did like you as a roommate. You were very entertaining!"

Leona snorted. "Glad I could amuse you, Ophelia." She shook her head. "But I really liked you."

"You mean you felt sorry for me," said Ophelia. "And

I can't blame you. I was told to act pathetic so everyone would feel bad for me and open up to me." She smiled. "I'm a really good actress, huh?"

Scarlet sneered. "A regular Rancora," she said.

"Who?" asked Adora loudly. Clearly she had missed the sound of her own voice.

"My old roommate, Mira, told me all about her," Scarlet explained. "She was a Starling Academy student and apparently quite the actress back in the day."

"Are you serious, guys?" said Cassie. "We're discussing this now?" She addressed Ophelia. "Here's what I want to know. Who did the holo-communications come from?"

The room grew silent. Everyone leaned forward.

Ophelia gave a sharp laugh. "They came from Lady Stella, of course."

Glossary

Afterglow: The Starling afterlife. When Starlings die, it is said that they have "begun their afterglow."

Age of Fulfillment: The age at which a Starling is considered mature enough to begin to study wish granting.

Bad Wish Orbs: Orbs that are the result of bad or selfish wishes made on Wishworld. These grow dark and warped and are quickly sent to the Negative Energy Facility.

Big Dipper Dormitory: Where third- and fourth-year students live.

Bot-Bot: A Starland robot. There are Bot-Bot guards, waiters, deliverers, and guides on Starland.

Bright Day: The date a Starling is born, celebrated each year like a Wishling birthday.

Celestial Café: Starling Academy's outstanding cafeteria.

Cocomoon: A sweet and creamy fruit with an iridescent glow.

Cosmic Transporter: The moving sidewalk system that transports students through dorms and across the Starling Academy campus.

Countdown Clock: A timing device on a Starling's Star-Zap. It lets them know how much time is left on a Wish Mission, which coincides with when the Wish Orb will fade.

Crystal Mountains: The most beautiful mountains on Starland. They are located across the lake from Starling Academy.

Cycle of Life: A Starling's life span. When Starlings die, they are said to have "completed their Cycle of Life."

Eternium wool: Fine strands of a strong, hard thread matted into a ball and used to scrub things clean. A bit like Wishworld steel wool.

Floozel: A Starland unit of distance similar to a Wishworld mile.

Glion: A gentle Starland creature similar in appearance to a Wishworld lion but with a multicolored glowing mane.

Good Wish Orbs: Orbs that are the result of positive wishes made on Wishworld. They are planted in Wish-Houses.

Halo Hall: The building where Starling Academy classes are held.

Holo-text: A message received on a Star-Zap and projected into the air. There are also holo-albums, holo-billboards, holo-books, holo-cards, holo-communications, holo-diaries, holo-flyers, holo-letters, holo-papers, holo-pictures, and holo–place cards. Anything that would be made of paper or contain writing or images on Wishworld is a hologram on Starland.

Hydrong: The equivalent of a Wishworld hundred.

Illumination Library: The impressive library at Starling Academy.

Impossible Wish Orbs: Orbs that are the result of wishes made on Wishworld that are beyond the power of Starlings to grant.

Lightning Lounge: A place on the Starling Academy campus where students relax and socialize.

Little Dipper Dormitory: Where first- and second-year students live.

Lolofruit: A large round fruit with a thick skin and juicy, aromatic flesh.

Luminous Lake: A serene and lovely lake next to the Starling Academy campus.

Mirror Mantra: A saying specific to each Star Darling that when recited gives her (and her Wisher) reassurance and strength. When a Starling recites her Mirror Mantra while looking in a mirror, she will see her true appearance reflected.

Moonberry: A fruit that is a lot like a blueberry, but with a more intense flavor.

Mooncheese crisp: A crunchy, savory Starland snack.

Moonium: An amount similar to a Wishworld million.

Old Prism: A medium-sized historical city about an hour from Starling Academy.

Power Crystal: The powerful stone that each Star Darling receives once she has granted her first wish.

Prickly buds: Buds from a Starland plant that are covered in a rough, prickly casing before they open.

Ruffruff tree: A Starland tree with rough, scratchy leaves.

Serenity Islands: A Starland recreation area. Starlings sometimes take paddleboat rides around it.

Shooting stars: Speeding stars that Starlings can latch on to and ride to Wishworld.

Silver Blossom: The final manifestation of a Good Wish Orb. This glimmering metallic bloom is placed in the Hall of Granted Wishes.

Sparkle shower: An energy shower Starlings take every day to get clean and refresh their sparkling glow.

Star ball: An intramural sport that shares similarities with soccer on Wishworld. Star ball players use energy manipulation to control the ball.

Starcar: The primary mode of transportation for most Starlings. These ultrasafe vehicles drive themselves on cushions of wish energy.

Star Caves: The caverns underneath Starling Academy where the Star Darlings' secret Wish-Cavern is located.

Stardominoes: Starland rectangular holo–game pieces that can be set up for a chain reaction in which they all knock each other over when one stardomino is knocked over.

Starf!: A Starling expression of dismay.

Star flash: News bulletin, often used sarcastically.

Star Kindness Day: A special Starland holiday that celebrates spreading kindness, compliments, and good cheer.

Starland City: The largest city on Starland, also its capital.

Starlicious: Tasty, delicious.

Starlings: The glowing beings with sparkly skin who live on Starland.

Starmarble: A very hard, glimmering Starland stone that is used as a building material.

Star Quad: The center of the Starling Academy campus. The dancing fountain, band shell, and hedge maze are located here.

Star salutations: The Starling way to say "thank you."

Starshoot: A Starland sport similar to Wishworld baseball, but players make use of energy manipulation techniques to move the ball.

Starweek: The Starland week, which is made up of eight star-days. The stardays in order are Sweetday, Shineday, Dododay, Yumday, Lunaday, Bopday, Reliquaday, and Babsday.

Staryear: The equivalent of a Wishworld year.

Star-Zap: The ultimate smartphone that Starlings use for all communications. It has myriad features.

Stellation: The point of a star. Halo Hall has five stellations, each housing a different department.

Supernova: A stellar explosion. Also used colloquially, meaning "really angry," as in "She went supernova when she found out the bad news."

Time of Letting Go: One of the four seasons on Starland. It falls between the warmest season and the coldest, similar to fall on Wishworld.

Time of Lumiere: The warmest season on Starland, similar to summer on Wishworld.

Time of New Beginnings: Similar to spring on Wishworld, this is the season that follows the coldest time of year; it's when plants and trees come into bloom.

Time of Shadows: The coldest season of the year on Starland, similar to winter on Wishworld.

Toothlight: A high-tech gadget that Starlings use to clean their teeth.

Vanisholine: A Starland natural substance used for cleaning.

Wish Blossom: The bloom that appears from a Wish Orb after its wish is granted.

Wish energy: The positive energy that is released when a wish is granted. Wish energy powers everything on Starland.

Wisher: The Wishling who has made the wish that is being granted.

Wish-Granters: Starlings whose job is to travel down to Wishworld to help make wishes come true and collect wish energy.

Wish-House: The place where Wish Orbs are planted and cared for until they sparkle. Once the orb's wish is granted, it becomes a Wish Blossom.

Wishlings: The inhabitants of Wishworld.

Wish Mission: The task a Starling undertakes when she travels to Wishworld to help grant a wish.

Wish Orb: The form a wish takes on Wishworld before traveling to Starland. There it will grow and sparkle when it's time to grant the wish.

Wish Pendant: A gadget that absorbs and transports wish energy, helps Starlings locate their Wishers, and changes a Starling's appearance. Each Wish Pendant holds a different special power for its Star Darling.

Wishworld: The planet Starland relies on for wish energy. The beings on Wishworld know it by another name—Earth.

Wishworld Outfit Selector: A program on each Star-Zap that accesses Wishworld fashions for Starlings to wear to blend in on their Wish Missions.

Wishworld Surveillance Deck: A platform located high above the campus, where Starling Academy students go to observe Wishlings through high-powered telescopes.

Zing: A traditional Starling breakfast drink. It can be enjoyed hot or iced.

Acknowledgments

It is impossible to list all of our gratitude, but we will try.

Our most precious gift and greatest teacher, Halo; we love you more than there are stars in the sky . . . punashaku. To the rest of our crazy, awesome, unique tribe—thank you for teaching us to go for our dreams. Integrity. Strength. Love. Foundation. Family. Grateful. Mimi Muldoon—from your star doodling to naming our Star Darlings, your artistry, unconditional love, and inspiration is infinite. Didi Muldoon—your belief and support in us is only matched by your fierce protection and massive-hearted guidance. Gail. Queen G. Your business sense and witchy wisdom are legendary. Frank—you are missed and we know you are watching over us all. Along with Tutu, Nana, and Deda, who are always present, gently guiding us in spirit. To our colorful, totally genius, and bananas siblings—Patrick, Moon, Diva, and Dweezil—there is more creativity and humor in those four names than most people experience in a lifetime. Blessed. To our magical nieces—Mathilda, Zola, Ceylon, and Mia—the Star Darlings adore you and so do we. Our witchy cuzzie fairy godmothers—Ane and Gina. Our fairy fashion godfather, Paris. Our sweet Panay. Teeta and Freddy—we love you all so much. And our four-legged fur babies—Sandwich, Luna, Figgy, and Pinky Star.

The incredible Barry Waldo, our SD partner. Sent to us from above in perfect timing. Your expertise and friendship are beyond words. We love you and Gary to the moon and back. Long live the manifestation room!

Catherine Daly—the stars shined brightly upon us the day we aligned with you. Your talent and inspiration are otherworldly; our appreciation cannot be expressed in words. Many heartfelt hugs for you and the adorable Oonagh.

To our beloved Disney family. Thank you for believing in us. Wendy Lefkon, our master guide and friend through this entire journey. Stephanie Lurie, for being the first to believe in Star Darlings. Suzanne Murphy, who helped every step of the way. Jeanne Mosure, we fell in love with you the first time we met, and Star Darlings wouldn't be what it is without you. Andrew Sugerman, thank you so much for all your support.

Our team . . . Devon (pony pants) and our Monsterfoot crew—so grateful. Richard Scheltinga—our angel and protector. Chris Abramson—thank you! Special appreciation to Richard Thompson, John LaViolette, Swanna, Mario, and Sam.

To our friends old and new—we are so grateful to be on this rad journey that is life with you all. Fay. Jorja. Chandra. Sananda. Sandy. Kathryn. Louise. What wisdom and strength you share. Ruth, Mike, and the rest of our magical Wagon Wheel bunch—how lucky we are. How inspiring you are. We love you.

Last—we have immeasurable gratitude for every person we've met along our journey, for all the good and the bad; it is all a gift. From the bottom of our hearts we thank you for touching our lives.

Shana Muldoon Zappa is a jewelry designer and writer who was born and raised in Los Angeles. She has an endless imagination and a passion to inspire positivity through her many artistic endeavors. She and her husband, Ahmet Zappa, collaborated on Star Darlings especially for their magical little girl and biggest inspiration, Halo Violetta Zappa.

Ahmet Zappa is the *New York Times* best-selling author of *Because I'm Your Dad* and *The Monstrous Memoirs of a Mighty McFearless*. He writes and produces films and television shows and loves pancakes, unicorns, and making funny faces for Halo and Shana.

Sneak Peek
Tessa's
Lost and Found

The next morning should have worked out perfectly for Tessa. All the Star Darlings were coming to her and Adora's room for an important meeting. And she was totally prepared.

Even though she'd stayed up late working on her holo-paper—and excuse note—Tessa had set the alarm on her Star-Zap for an extra-early wake-up time. Before morning, the alarm buzzed her favorite childhood tune, "Old MacStarlight Had a Farm."

She took her sparkle shower in record time, not losing track of starmins the way she usually did. She finished so quickly, in fact, Adora was still sleeping soundly when she went back to the room.

So Tessa tidied her ultra-plush bedcovers and smoothed her soft-as-a-cloud rug. Both came from Bed, Bath, and Beyond the Stars' exclusive line of luxury items, perfect for Tessa, who liked to surround herself with sumptuous comfort.

Then she pulled on the outfit she'd laid out the night before: an emerald-green and ocean-blue striped sweaterdress that swirled around her knees. It matched Tessa's long wavy hair perfectly.

Quickly, Tessa checked her Star-Zap to make sure she was still on schedule. Yes, she was doing great. She picked up her starbrush to brush her sweeping bangs to the side. There was just one more thing to accomplish before the Star Darlings came over. She just had to—

Tessa caught sight of the headboard over her bed . . . and everything fell apart.

The headboard was really one big holo-screen, and Tessa was drawn to it like metal to a magnet.

Initially, Tessa had used the screen to care for virtual pets. She loved creatures of all sizes, shapes, and glows. But then she'd programmed the screen to show her family farm in real time—real creatures in real action.

Tessa and her younger sister, Gemma—also a Star Darling—were from Solar Springs, a tiny town of gently rolling hills. A small number of families lived on simple farms nestled in valleys. It was a lovely spot. But the town had just one general store that sold only basic items, like toothlights and starbrushes.

When Tessa wanted that starmazing luster-lotion for her skin, or the glitz gloves that felt soft as shimmer-butter, she had to put in a special order. Except for that, Tessa loved her farm life: the fresh fruits and vegetables she used for cooking, the farm creatures . . .

And that was why she couldn't turn away from the screen. Her favorite creature of all, a playful baby galliope named Jewel, was there in all her cuteness, nudging a round druderwomp bush across the ground like a ball.

The deep purple galliope was all spindly legs and long neck, with a glowing feathery mane and tail. Tessa had seen holo-pictures of Wishworld ponies. She agreed they resembled galliopes. But she doubted they could hold a glowstick to Jewel in charm alone.

Tessa dropped her starbrush and edged closer to the holo-screen. "Jewel," she cooed softly. "Star salutations, little girl."

If Jewel was in the right mood, she could step out of the screen—or at least her image could—and be virtually close to Tessa. Hoping that would happen then, Tessa tapped the bottom of the screen, and a virtual star-apple floated into her hand. She held the sparkling round fruit out to Jewel. Back on the farm, it wouldn't be just an image; the star-apple would be real and crunchy and sweet.

Jewel whinnied, stepped out of the screen, and nuzzled Tessa's neck. "I could do this all starday," Tessa said with a giggle.

"Maybe you could, but you really shouldn't," said Adora. Tessa looked across the room. Adora had gotten up and dressed without her even noticing.

"Everyone will be here in a starsec. So pick up your starbrush and finish getting ready."

Tessa ignored her, putting her arm around Jewel. "I don't like being told what to do," she whispered, as if the galliope could understand. "You'd think after rooming together for so long, Adora would know that."

Sighing, Adora picked up Tessa's starbrush and placed it on the nightstand. "Come on, Tessa, I put away all my test tubes and experiments—even that new lip-sparkle I'm working on. The one that actually shoots out sparks."

Adora spoke as calmly as ever; Tessa had rarely seen her ruffled or emotional. And they generally got along. But Tessa had cleaned up! What was one little starbrush in the grand scheme of things? Still, the Star Darlings were coming over. . . .

Tessa waved good-bye to Jewel, and the galliope stepped back into the screen. "See you soon, little girl. Next time we'll play and we'll—"

"Starland to Tessa!" Adora snapped her fingers in front of Tessa's face. "The Star Darlings meeting is—"

"Knock-knock," sang Leona from the other side of the door.

"Now!" Adora finished, nodding toward the door so it slid open quickly. The other ten Star Darlings walked into the room and settled on beds, chairs, and rugs.

"Oh, Tessa," Gemma said, disappointment in her voice. She eyed Tessa's cleared-off table. "I thought for sure you'd have a whole breakfast spread for us."

Tessa groaned. That was what she'd been planning to do! Before she was distracted by Jewel, she had been about to bake breakfast treats in the micro-zap!

Scarlet shook her head emphatically, her dark hood falling to her shoulders before she quickly pulled it back up. "Breakfast is not important," she said brusquely. "We'll have plenty of time to go to the Celestial Café after the meeting."

"Still, we could have met a little later," Piper said wistfully, covering up a yawn. Tessa knew Piper liked her rest more than the average Starling.

"No, meeting now makes the most sense," said Vega.

"This way we take care of business and keep the rest of the starday free for studying."

"I would have voted for a bit later so I'd have had time to warm up my vocal cords." Leona's voice started out deep, then rose higher with every word: "Now I have to do my exercises in regular conversation."

"Please, spare us," Scarlet said.

Tessa sighed. Those roommates were a much bigger mismatch than she and Adora! She doubted they would ever get along.

Cassie held up a hand, and everyone quieted down. She was the smallest Starling of the group, but her words carried great weight. "The fact is, spies could be any-where on campus. I don't know whom we can even trust! We had to meet this early so no one would see us."

Libby stood up. "Okay, everybody, let's stop talking about meeting and actually meet!"

Tessa agreed. This was taking way too long, and without her usual pre-breakfast snack, she was hungry.

"Right." Cassie nodded. She took off her star-shaped glasses, polished them so they shone, and nodded again. "There is one basic question we need to answer: who is behind all these crazy problems—"

"Like our holo-text compliments coming out as insults," interrupted Piper indignantly.

"And every student invited to try out for my band," Leona added, "when it should have just been Star Darlings! That could have broken up our group!"

"And those are just communication issues," Cassie continued. "What about everything else? The poisonous flowers? The strange nail polish that wouldn't come off? Who is responsible?"

"It's so obvious," Scarlet huffed, "any wee Starling could figure it out."

Everyone turned to her, curious.

"It's Lady Stella."

Tessa gasped, along with some of the other Star Darlings. *How could Scarlet think that, even for a starsec?* she wondered.

Lady Stella was the head of the school. She was revered in academic circles for her principles and forward thinking in education. She was held in highest regard all across Starland. Business Starlings, Starling scientists, and heads of state constantly consulted her, and wee Starlings wanted to grow up to be just like her.

Tessa had actually dressed as Lady Stella once for Light Giving Day (it had been that or a moonberry), when young Starlings dressed in costume to hand out flowers and welcome the growing season. She guessed many others in the room had, too.

Tessa thought back to one of her first days at the academy, well before the Star Darlings had been formed. She had been curled up in a chair in the Lightning Lounge, holo-texting Gemma back home and feeling homesick.

Lady Stella had come over and sat down next to her. She seemed to know all about Tessa without Tessa's saying a word, and she led her on a tour of the Celestial Café kitchen, where Bot-Bot cooks and waitstaff worked.

"You can come here any time you like," she had said, "and cook, bake, or just relax. The Bot-Bots will be informed."

Then they'd sat in a corner and munched on moonberries together. It turned out to be Lady Stella's favorite snack, too.

Lady Stella couldn't be capable of any wrongdoing whatsoever!

"Scarlet, you're going galactic!" said Libby, apparently agreeing. "The evil Starling doesn't even have to be part of Starling Academy! He or she could be from outside the school."

"I doubt that," Cassie said nervously. "Whoever is doing this would need to be here full-time. And Lady Stella is here 36/8."

"You're both going galactic!" Sage said to Scarlet and

Cassie. "Lady Stella has been starmendous to each and every one of us!"

"Well, count me out of that lucky star group," Scarlet shot back. "Here's a fact for you, Lady Flip My Hair Dramatically Because I'm So Startacular I Was Chosen for the First Wish Mission: my grades were switched with dimwit Ophelia's, so I was kicked out of the Star Darlings. Who else would be able to do that?"

The girls fell silent. It was hard to disagree with Scarlet; she could so easily go supernova. Tessa looked at Leona, who stood up to her regularly. But Leona had been uncharacteristically quiet. Then Tessa glanced at Gemma. What was her sister thinking? She, too, had been quiet.

"Well, lots of Starlings could have access to records," Tessa finally said. "What about the groundskeeper who checks that the disappearing garbage pails are working properly? He goes into every room on campus."

Gemma finally spoke up. "That's right! Once, when I was walking past the teachers' lounge, I was hurrying really fast down the hall. I can't even remember why I was there. Maybe because I had to go to the Radiant Rec Center and I was a little nervous because I had never—"

"Get to the point of the story," said Scarlet.

"Well, the groundskeeper was outside the lounge

door, stooping over. He could have been trying to listen in!"

"Or fix the hand scanner," said Scarlet.

"Besides, he has no idea what's what," Astra added. "Once, he asked where the star ball field was, and he was standing right in front of the goal!"

"Lady Cordial keeps close watch of all the comings and goings in that hall," Cassie noted, "because the admissions office is there. She'd notice anything strange. So forget about the groundskeeper!" She sighed. "Lady Stella must have set up the whole Scarlet-Ophelia switch. She told me Ophelia was an orphan. She lied. Ophelia was never even in an orphanage!"

Scarlet leaned closer to Sage with an almost compassionate expression. "I was fooled, too, for a long time." A shadow passed over her face. "But she pulled the glimmersilk over my eyes."

Finally, Leona spoke up, as if she'd been weighing the information and had made up her mind. "The biggest piece of evidence is Ophelia herself. She came right out and said Lady Stella had sent the holo-mails asking her to come to Starling Academy and pretend to be a Star Darling. Poor girl, she wanted to be a student here so much she was willing to try—and who could blame her? Especially once she was rooming with me."

"But why would Lady Stella want to sabotage our missions?" Vega asked. "It doesn't make sense. The missions were her idea to begin with!"

The girls all spoke at once.

"Maybe she changed her mind and wants to end the Star Darlings. But she doesn't want to hurt our feelings."

"Maybe she wants Starling Academy to fail so she can start a new school."

"Maybe she wants to move to Wishworld!"

"Maybe she's in love with the groundskeeper and they're running off together!"

"Maybe she's just a hologram, and the real Lady Stella is being held captive in one of the underground caves."

Tessa shivered. Piper's last comment was especially creepy.

"I don't know why she's doing it," said Scarlet. "But we have to confront her, and soon."

"I just don't believe it," said Tessa stubbornly. "I need real proof."

"I don't believe it, either," Sage said.

"Well, isn't your family—at least your mother—really close with her?" Scarlet asked Sage.

Sage's mother was a renowned energy scientist, and Lady Stella had consulted with her many times.

"What!" Sage opened her lavender eyes wide in surprise. "You're not seriously accusing my mother of sabotage?"

The room fell silent. The girls eyed each other nervously. No one knew what to say. But then Tessa's stomach rumbled loudly. Gemma laughed, breaking the tension.

"I say we've talked enough for now. It's time to eat," said Tessa.

Cassie nodded and stood up. "Before we confront anyone," she said to Scarlet, "we should do more sleuthing." Then she turned to Tessa. "And you're right, of course. We should all go to breakfast."

Cassie is smart, Tessa thought as everyone left the room, *even if she does suspect Lady Stella. And she's read all those detective books her uncle wrote; she must know about sleuthing.* She'd stick close to Cassie, find out what was really going on, and put in her two stars to defend Lady Stella whenever she could.

Tessa stepped onto the Cosmic Transporter, careful to get in place right behind the younger Starling.

Cassie and Scarlet were standing side by side, whispering. Tessa edged closer, trying to listen. *It's not like I'm really eavesdropping*, she reasoned. *We're all just heading to the Celestial Café at the same time.*

"Mumble, mumble Lady Stella," she heard. "Mumble mumble Leona." "Mumble Ophelia." "Mumble mumble mumble."

Nothing new there.

Then Cassie said "Star Caves" loud and clear. Scarlet gave her a "shut your stars" look. "Later!" she whispered harshly.

Hmmm, thought Tessa. Now that was interesting. They must think the secret underground tunnels, where the special Star Darlings Wish Cavern was hidden, held clues. *Maybe*—

Suddenly, the star above the Celestial Café dimmed, signaling that breakfast was about to end. Tessa forgot about the caves. She took off past the other Starlings, thoughts of warm astromuffins and sparkle toast filling her head.